THE OWNER OF HIS HEART

Published by Amorous Publishing

http://theodorataylor.com/

Copyright ☐ 2011 Theodora Taylor

ISBN: # **9781470195526**

ALL RIGHTS RESERVED

WARNING: The unauthorized reproduction or distribution of this copyrighted work is illegal. No part of this book may be used or reproduced electronically or in print without written permission, except in the case of brief quotations embodied in reviews.
This is a work of fiction. All names, characters, and places are fictitious. Any resemblance to actual events, locales, organizations, or persons, living or dead, is entirely coincidental.

CHAPTER ONE

LAYLA MATTHEWS had seen some off-putting work spaces in her lifetime. Back in Dallas, where she used to work before returning to Pittsburgh, she'd visited a few of her patients at offices housed in concrete buildings. But she had never seen anything as cold and sterile as the waiting room outside Nathan Sinclair's office. Though expensively decorated, the chrome furniture and large black and white framed industrial photos seemed to emit a cold wind. Layla shivered just thinking about confronting the man who sat behind the closed, black office door.

"Will it be much longer?" she asked his assistant

"Mr. Sinclair is on a call. When he gets off, I'll let him know you're here," the woman answered without looking up from her computer.

Layla eyed Sinclair's assistant—an overly thin brunette in her fifties who wore her hair in a tight bun. She patted her own messy curls, wishing she had gone home after her shift to change out of her scrubs and subdue her wild hair into a more business-like style. She shouldn't have rushed over here, even though she'd had an unexpected breakthrough in the mystery she'd come back to Pittsburgh to solve.

That morning, Layla had finally gotten around to sorting through her dead father's paperwork. She'd sifted through all his bills, setting aside the ones she hadn't known about and therefore hadn't managed to pay off yet. But then she found a piece of paper that wasn't a bill. To her great surprise, it was the receipt for a check made out to her father for more than what she earned in a year as a physical therapist and signed

The Owner of His Heart

by someone named Nathan Sinclair. It was dated just a short time after her accident.

Layla immediately got on her computer, searching for Nathan Sinclair and Pittsburgh. Several hits came back identifying him as the current CEO of Sinclair Industries, a family-owned steel company. Unfortunately, she hadn't had time to learn anything else about him other than his job title, because she had to get to work. But she'd been so excited about stumbling upon her first clue, she'd barely made it through her shift, much less thought about going home first to change, before heading to the Sinclair Industries downtown offices.

But now she'd been waiting for almost an hour in Nathan Sinclair's sleek, modern outer office. She grabbed a black scrunchie out of her purse and pulled her hair into a simple knot. It made her feel a little better, however the longer she waited, the more out of place she felt in her purple scrubs and lime green Crocs. How had her father, a compulsive gambler, who had never been able to hold on to a job for more than six months, even known the steel magnate anyway? And why would a man in Sinclair's position write someone like her father such a large check?

His assistant interrupted her musings with a clipped pronouncement: "Ms. Matthews, it's now six o'clock, Mr. Sinclair's cut-off for seeing unannounced visitors." She peered at Layla from behind her large chrome desk. "I'm afraid you'll have to go now."

"What?" Layla couldn't believe the woman had let her wait this long only to kick her out. "I hate to be rude, but did you even tell him I was here?"

The assistant pursed her lips. "Like I said, he's on a conference call and I see no reason to disturb him. If you like, I can make an appointment for you, to guarantee you'll be able to see him at a later date." She turned to her computer and opened up what Layla assumed must be Nathan Sinclair's calendar. "I have a 10 o'clock available for August seventeenth.

Layla's heart sank. It was early May. "Would you terribly mind telling him I'm here? My name is Layla Matthews. I'm the daughter of Henry Matthews."

The assistant leveled a cool glance on her. "Ms. Matthews, you showed up here out of the blue. This is the only appointment I have available right now. Would you like it or not?"

Thick desperation began building up inside her. This was Layla's first big break in her case. She couldn't wait until August to talk to Mr. Sinclair. "Please, just tell him I'm here. It won't take long, I promise. I only have a couple of questions for him."

"A lot of women just want to 'talk' to Mr. Sinclair," the assistant said. "If you really have business with him, you can make an appointment. Or would you like me to call security? That can also be arranged."

The woman tilted her body towards her large, black desk phone as if to signal that she wasn't making empty threats.

Layla, in turn, sighed and said, "Oh, I'm so sorry..." she gave the assistant an apologetic grimace, "...for making you call security."

Then without any further warning, she dashed toward the black door.

***

Nathan Sinclair had been on the phone with his

brother, Andrew, for over an hour, trying to convince him to come home from...wherever he was.

"Is it Ibiza?" Nathan asked. "Your Spanish was always pretty good."

"No," his brother answered, sounding glum. "It doesn't matter where I am. I'm not coming home."

"This doesn't make the company look good, Andrew. The Sinclair Ball is in a few months, and people will talk if Diana ends up hosting it alone."

"Let them talk," his brother said. "When did you start caring about what other people think anyway? You used to be the bad boy, and now look at you."

Nathan rubbed a hand over his tired face. "You're the head of our Global Initiatives team. You're the one who brought Matsuda Steel to the table, and Matsuda just confirmed he'll be attending the ball this year. So if we're serious about partnering with them for a Tokyo site, we need to look like a strong, united family—not a soap opera with a missing brother and a wife who can't say for sure where he is. What will it look like if you're not there?"

"I've tried to make it work with Diana, I have," his brother said, ignoring Nathan's valid question. "But she's not the one for me."

"Fine," Nathan said. "I don't care. But can you tell her that after the ball? I don't want all of Pittsburgh gossiping about your divorce when Matsuda comes through."

"Wow, way to be sympathetic," Andrew said. "It's good you work in steel, because you have a lot in common with our main product."

A good brother would have pretended to feel even a little bit contrite. But Andrew had disappeared over a week ago and was only just now calling to let him know he was still alive. Also, Nathan had never been a particularly good brother.

"I don't care where you are or what you're going through. Be back for the ball, or else."

"Or else, what?" his brother asked, clearly wanting to be issued an official ultimatum, which Nathan would be more than happy to give. Their relationship had always been like this, contentious and competitive. One of his earliest memories was being pulled off of Andrew by a servant during one of the many fistfights they'd had as kids.

But before he could tell his brother exactly what kind of hell he'd bring down if Andrew didn't come home in time for the ball, Nathan's door banged open and then slammed shut.

"What the—" Nathan broke off when he saw who was now standing with her back pressed to his door. She was maybe ten pounds heavier under the ridiculous purple scrubs, and her hair was much longer, but he recognized her in an instant. It was Layla Matthews, a woman he hadn't seen in nearly a decade. A woman who he still hated with every fiber of his being.

CHAPTER TWO

"I'LL have to call you back," Nathan said to his brother.

"How will you call me back if you don't know where I am?" his brother asked.

But Nathan just hung up. He dropped the receiver in its cradle without taking his eyes off of his unexpected guest.

"Come out of there, young lady," Kate, his assistant, yelled from the other side of the door. "Security is on their way, and we'll have you forcibly removed."

Layla gave him an apologetic smile and held up a finger. "Hold on just a moment, please," she said. Then she turned her attention to the door's locking apparatus.

He stared at her, taking in everything from her springy black curls, barely held back by an overburdened scrunchie, to her large, almond-shaped brown eyes, which were crinkled with chagrin. Her mouth, though free of lipstick, remained as lush and inviting as ever. And her nose, which was a little large, made her dark face more striking than gorgeous.

Nathan tended to date gorgeous women, but at that moment he couldn't tear his eyes away from Layla. He felt himself harden. Even after what she'd done, his desire for her couldn't be regulated by logic.

After some fiddling, she managed to lock the door. She paused and took a moment to regain her composure before approaching his desk. Layla held her hand out towards him.

"Hi, I'm Layla Matthews," she said.

He stood but made no move to shake her hand.

"Henry Matthews daughter," she said, as if he needed another reminder of who she was.

"I know who you are," he said. "My question is, what are you doing here?"

***

Layla didn't know what she'd been expecting when she barged into Nathan Sinclair's office, but it hadn't been the man she found behind a large metal desk.

She had thought Nathan Sinclair would be like most CEOs—clean-cut, older, with gray hair, and wearing a black business suit. But the man behind the desk was not only exceedingly handsome, he looked to be just a little older than her own twenty-eight years. And though she could see a black jacket hanging on his hawkish executive chair, he wasn't wearing a tie, and the top two buttons of his crisp, white button-up shirt were open, allowing it to stretch across his broad chest in a very unbusiness-like way. Also, unlike the CEO she had imagined, he wore his sable brown hair slightly too long with about three days worth of unchecked beard growth.

But what really made her uneasy were his grey eyes. They lasered in on her when she entered the room, and became downright cold when she approached his desk.

"I know who you are," he said, ignoring her outstretched hand. "My question is what are you doing here?"

"Oh," she said, scrambling to reset. "You know who I am? Do we—I mean, did we know each other?"

Something flashed in his cold grey eyes. "Are you attempting to make fun of me? Is this a joke?"

"No," Layla said. She lowered her hand. "I had an accident. Maybe you knew or heard about it. I fell down some stairs and ended up in a two-day coma. But when I woke up, I'd lost a year."

"A year," he repeated, suspicion lacing his voice.

"Yes, my entire time in Pittsburgh—I don't remember anything." She rushed into an explanation. "All I know is I moved here from New Orleans to attend college before I had my accident. But when I woke up from the coma, I didn't remember any of it. My dad moved me back to New Orleans, and after years of physical therapy, I ended up going to school in Dallas to become a physical therapist myself. But now I'm back, and I'm sorry, but I don't remember you."

She wrung her hands together. "In fact, I'm trying to figure out how we would have even come in contact. And why did you give my father money? Was it a loan?"

He leaned forward and stared at her so hard Layla felt like he was running an unseen lie detector scan over her. "You're serious," he said. "You don't remember me or anything that happened while you were here?"

"I tried to ask my father, but he just kept saying it was better that I didn't remember. He died a few months ago."

Layla paused, waiting for him to extend his condolences but he said nothing. "I suppose you two weren't friends, then."

"No, we weren't friends."

Layla hated this, hated being at such a disadvantage. She kept asking questions, but his answers only confused her more. Plus, the way he was looking at her set something akin to terror off in her heart. Run! her primitive instincts screamed at her, but another part of her insisted she get her answers no matter how much he scared her.

"Did we know each other?" she asked again.

"What do you want?" he asked. "Why are you here?"

With trembling fingers she pulled the receipt out of her purse. "I found this," she said, forcing herself to hand him the piece of paper.

He snatched it, looked at it, looked back at her, then tossed it on the desk. "Yes, and...?"

His officiousness began to annoy Layla and her fear ebbed away, replaced by anger. "You know, you don't have to act so hostile," she said. "I'm just trying to figure this all out."

More fists pounded on the office door. This time a male voice called out, "Security! Open the door! Mr. Sinclair, are you all right?"

Nathan Sinclair stared at her for a few hard beats, then surprised her by calling back, "Yes, I'm fine. Go away!"

There came many seconds of confused silence, then the guard asked, "Are you sure?"

"Yes, I'm sure. Now go away. I can handle her myself, and I don't need your services."

Layla cocked her head and gave him a censorious look. "You could be a little nicer. He's only trying to help." She called out to the security guard, "I'm so sorry for any trouble I caused you. Thank you for doing your job so well. Mr. Sinclair really appreciates it."

"No problem. Let me know if you need anything," the man on the other side of the door responded.

"We will. Thanks again," Layla replied. She turned

back to Nathan with a smile. "Pittsburghers are so friendly. I'm really loving it here."

Nathan Sinclair narrowed his eyes at her, putting her in mind of Clint Eastwood in those westerns her father used to watch. "Are you serious?"

"Yes, Pittsburgh is great."

"I mean about the security guard. I could have handled that situation without your interference."

Layla couldn't believe he was even arguing this point. "Thank you is the least we could say. He came all the way up here."

"Yes, because protecting me is what he gets paid to do. You don't have to thank people for doing their jobs."

"No, you don't have to," Layla said. "But it's a nice thing to do."

He folded his arms, his face becoming a work of stone. "You're still doing that, I see."

"Doing what?" she asked.

"Pretending to be nice. You're still keeping up with the good girl act."

"It's not an act as far as I know..." Layla took a tentative step toward the desk. "...but was I mean to you? Is that why you don't like me?"

"No, I dislike you for other reasons," he said. He picked up the receipt again. "This is money my father, the late Nathan Sinclair Sr., paid your father because he was threatening to sue our family."

"Threatening to sue you for what?" Layla asked.

"Those stairs you fell down were at our house. He said you would go to the press and say you were pushed if we didn't pay him."

Layla clutched a hand to her heart, hearing this. She wished she could say she was surprised. But her father had always had loose moral codes when it came to feeding his gambling habit. She could easily see him blackmailing Nathan Sinclair Sr. for a large amount of money, then gambling it all away on the New Orleans riverboats. She'd managed to eventually move out and make a fresh start in Dallas after her accident. But even after she moved, her father's many debts continued to haunt her. And three months after his funeral, she was still cleaning up his messes.

"I'll pay you back," she told him.

"What?" he said. His hard expression shifted from anger to curiosity. "How?"

"I don't know," she said. "In installments?"

Now he laughed, but it was a mean, dark sound, steeped in frank disbelief, which pissed Layla off. "I will pay you back. It might take a while, but I will. I'm sorry my father blackmailed yours."

He just shook his head, his eyes laced with disgust. "Like I said, still pretending. You're such a sweet girl, so good. That's what you've always wanted everyone to believe, isn't it?"

She stepped closer to his desk, her chin going up. "Listen," she said. "I told you I don't remember you."

"Convenient," he said, snarled really.

"It's the truth," she said, voice raised. "So either tell me how we know each other and why you're so angry at me or zip it."

Layla couldn't believe the words coming out of her mouth. To a certain extent, he was right about her. She tried her best to be nice, to be polite, to be all the things her father hadn't been. She had even gone into a helping profession. But there was something about Nathan Sinclair that upset her equilibrium. She didn't want to be nice to him. In fact, he irked her so bad, her palms itched to slap him.

Seconds ticked by as they took each other's measure. Him challenging her with his stare, her refusing to back down by lowering her eyes.

She thought she'd won the stare-off when he turned away from her. But then he grabbed a file folder out of one of his desk drawers, dropped the receipt into it, and said, "Fine, I'll expect you the second Friday of next month with the first installment."

She blinked. "You want me to deliver the check here?"

He held out his hand. "Right into my palm."

"I mean, couldn't I just deposit it into a bank account or something? Or maybe mail you the check?" The same instinct that had told her to run was now telling her she did not want to confront this man again. That she should do whatever it took to keep her distance.

He sat back down and steepled his hands in front of him.

"I like to look into my enemy's eyes when it comes to payback—even if in this case, my enemy is literally paying my family back. You'll come here, to this office, and hand me each check directly until you're done paying back every cent. Those are my terms. Either take them or you can—how did you put it? Zip it."

His tone was soft, but his eyes brooked no argument, and Layla knew he wouldn't be convinced to modify his so-called terms. His face was beautiful, but she could now see there was something very cruel inside of him. For some reason, he wanted to watch her suffer under the burden of repaying her father's debt.

"Fine," she said. She schooled her face into a

emotionless stare. She didn't want to give him the satisfaction of seeing the anxiety now churning in her stomach as she tried to figure out how to pay him back as quickly as possible. "I'll see you in June."

"Fine," he said. "You may go now."

With that, he took his laser gaze off of her and turned it to his computer.

"Thank you for meeting with me and for not handing me over to security," she said, because it was the polite thing to say. And she was determined to remain polite even if Nathan Sinclair couldn't appreciate such niceties.

He didn't answer, just typed on his keyboard, signaling he had already dismissed her before she was even out the door.

"Bye," she said, feeling silly now, but unable to stop herself from issuing one more small courtesy.

Again, he didn't answer. So she left, already piecing together a plan to get more hours at her physical therapy center. She'd work double shifts every day if it meant paying back that blackmail money sooner rather than later. Even though she still had a lot more questions, she had never wanted to be done with anything the way she wanted to be done with Nathan Sinclair.

***

Nathan waited ten minutes after the door clicked behind Layla to pick up the phone and buzz Kate.

"Yes, Mr. Sinclair?" she said, picking up immediately.

"That investigator we used for the Columbus

lawsuit..."

"Spencer Greeley?" she said.

"Yes, contract his services. I want him to get everything he can find on Layla Matthews. And I especially want access to her medical records."

She paused, obviously wondering what this was all about, but she was too professional to ask outright. In the end, she simply said, "Yes, Mr. Sinclair. I'll get right on that."

Nathan usually hung up after issuing his orders, but this time he stopped himself and said, "Thank you."

"You're welcome," his assistant replied, sounding rather startled.

He gritted his teeth and hung up. Layla Matthews had only been back in his life for a few minutes, but she was already disrupting it in ways he didn't like. Again. With her innocent doe eyes and the luscious curves hidden underneath those hideous scrubs... he couldn't help but want to pull them off, just to see how much that body of hers had changed in the nine years since they'd seen each other last.

He didn't know what her game was, or why she had come back to Pittsburgh, but he planned to find out and neutralize her before his brother returned. Just a few minutes ago, he had been furious with Andrew for skipping town, but now he could see what a stroke of luck that had been. If he played the situation right, he could get Layla Matthews to leave Pittsburgh before the ball, before Andrew came back, and before she figured out she and his brother used to be in love.

CHAPTER THREE

BY THE TIME the second Friday of June rolled around, Nathan began to see what a bad idea it had been to insist Layla meet with him in person to hand over her first installment. At the time, he'd done it to make her uncomfortable, him batting at her in their game of cat and mouse. But that had been before Spencer Greeley sent in his report and he'd discovered everything Layla had told him that day she barged into his office had been true.

According to Greeley's findings, after her fall and subsequent forty-eight-hour coma, Layla woke up unable to remember her accident, or anything that happened in the year prior to it, including moving to Pittsburgh to attend college, and meeting her boyfriend, Andrew. And since Andrew had never visited her in the hospital, there had been no reason for her to seek him out. His brother had been forbidden to see her by both their father and the family lawyers after Henry Matthews had threatened to sue them.

"Layla wants to sue you all," Henry had told Nathan, Andrew, and their father nine years ago when he visited the Sinclair mansion, ostensibly to let them know she had come out of her coma. They'd invited him to meet with them in the study, where Henry had confessed with much false handwringing that Layla wanted to sue the Sinclairs.

"She says maybe she was pushed down those stairs," Henry said. "I told her that couldn't be. She fell face forward, you see, and the doctors think she just slipped. But she told me to come here and tell you that. She thinks maybe you'll give her something to make sure this story don't get out."

Their father had not suffered this foolishness for long. "How much does she want?" he asked. He tended to be decisive and to the point when it came to business decisions. It was a quality Nathan had inherited from him, which was why his father had named him CEO in his will instead of his brother.

Henry named the price, and his father wrote down a number three times that amount on a piece of paper, which he slid across the desk.

"That's what we'll pay you. Once. I'm not as nice as my son, Andrew, here. Tell your daughter if she ever comes near him or tries to blackmail my family again, I won't hesitate to ensure it's the last time she does it. Do you understand?"

Henry's voice shook when he answered, "I understand. Layla don't have a bank account. Could you make that check out to me?"

Nathan had known Layla's father was a slime ball just from that one exchange, but according to Greeley's report, he'd been even worse than Nathan thought. He had gotten a job in New Orleans that would let him add his nineteen-year-old daughter to his insurance, then he had blown the money their father had paid him to gamble on the riverboats.

From what Nathan could tell, Layla hadn't seen a dime and had even taken out loans to complete her masters in physical therapy. He read through the report, which detailed how she grew up, with an itinerant gambler for a father, hopping from Las Vegas to Reno to New Orleans until she eventually landed at Carnegie Mellon, where she met his brother, only to lose any memory of having attended the prestigious university or her relationship with Andrew less than a year later.

Anyone else would have felt sorry for her, reading over this tragic backstory. But no one else knew the Layla Nathan knew. Not even his brother had known what she had really been like.

He could still remember the first time he saw her. He had been partying the night before and had woken up in some strange girl's room on the other side of town, so hung over he'd barely managed to crawl out of bed and into his Ferrari to get himself home to the family mansion. He didn't live in the main house like his brother, but had taken over the one-bedroom guest cottage out back, which unfortunately was gated off and could only be accessed by walking through the mansion.

He'd snuck in through the kitchen to avoid his parents, who, back in those days, needed very little prompting to start asking when he planned to do something with his life and why he couldn't be more like his brother. But when he walked in through the back door, he found a large-eyed black girl with closely-cropped hair and a pretty face, sitting at the kitchen table, a chemistry textbook spread out in front of her.

"Hi," she said, giving him a toothy smile after he came stumbling in. "You must be Nathan."

His hangover headache intensified. "Yeah, I'm Nathan. Who are you?"

"I'm Layla."

He dropped into a seat across from her and commanded, "Get me some coffee. Now."

She just sat there, observing him in his pain.

"I said coffee," he repeated.

"Please," she said.

"What?" he asked.

"You forgot to say please."

He blinked at her. "Who are you?"

"I'm Layla," she said again.

"No, who are you to me? Are you one of the servants? No, you're too young. One of their daughters? Is that why you won't fetch?"

"You have so many servants, you don't know anything about their family members?" she asked.

"No, that's not it. Maybe I've seen you before, maybe I haven't. I just didn't care enough to remember you until you came between me and my coffee."

She closed her large textbook and said, "What if I was one of the servants' daughters? Would you have her or him fired just because I didn't get your cup of coffee?"

He narrowed his eyes at her. "That depends. If you get me coffee now that you know what the situation is, then no, I won't fire your mother or father. If you don't…" He let the threat hang in the air.

"Wow," she said. Then she expelled a breath of air, before she picked up the thick textbook, held it high above her head, and dropped it. The resulting bang against the kitchen table sent a piercing pain arcing through the back of his brain.

He groaned. "What are you doing?"

"My mother's dead and thank goodness my father doesn't work here," she yelled at the top of her lungs. "So I'm taking advantage of the fact that you can't fire them because I won't fetch."

Her yelling had the equivalent effect of beating drumsticks against his throbbing head. "Shut up," he commanded.

"Make me!" she shouted back. "Make me you

ridiculous, arrogant, spoiled, rich boy!"

Nathan covered his ears, trying to block out her voice. But then it turned out he didn't have to. Footsteps sounded from the other room, and Layla's head jerked up, like an animal that had caught the scent of another.

She picked up the book and scrambled back into her chair with it, opening it to the page she had been studying before Nathan had come in through the back door.

By the time Andrew entered the kitchen, dressed in jeans and a light blue polo, Layla was the very picture of someone studying peacefully.

"Seriously, bro," he said, upon seeing Nathan. "It's ten in the morning and you smell like the Yuengling distillery."

Yuengling was a local beer, and it happened to be exactly what Nathan had been drinking in copious amounts the night before. But Nathan was too furious with Layla to respond to his brother's insult. He pointed at Layla, his head throbbing even worse than before. "Who is she?" he demanded. "And what the hell is she doing here?"

"This is Layla," his brother said. "She's tutoring me in chemistry."

Nathan's eyes narrowed. "You're going into the family business. What do you care about chemistry?"

Layla looked up at him, confused, and Andrew blushed. "I've always liked chemistry," he said, despite his red face.

Nathan turned back to Layla. "Where did he find you?"

"In the school academic development office," she said. "He came in for peer counseling."

"How old are you?" Nathan asked.

"I'm eighteen," she answered.

"And he's a twenty-one-year-old junior, who supposedly needs a freshman's help in chemistry. A really cute freshman's help. Yeah right. He just split up with his girlfriend and now he's trying to get laid." He turned back to his brother. "You probably aren't even taking chemistry. No room for it on your business major schedule, right?"

Andrew didn't answer, but the deeper shade of red he turned was answer enough. Nathan stood up. "Well, good luck with this harpy. If you see a servant, tell her to bring some coffee to the guest house."

He left the kitchen on the high note of having blown his goody-two-shoes brother's cover story.

But Layla even managed to thwart him in this. The last thing he heard her say before he left the room was, "It's okay, Andrew. Actually, it's kind of sweet…"

Less than two weeks later, they were officially dating, much to the consternation of their parents who had much preferred Andrew's ex-girlfriend, Diana Swinton, a society blond, and the daughter of another prominent Pittsburgh business family.

But no one had disapproved of the relationship more than Nathan, who knew from the start what she was really like. He also knew he'd gone hard the moment he'd seen her sitting at the table, and he'd stayed that way for hours after that, until he jerked himself off, with visions of her underneath him, calling his name and begging him for more.

Now nine years later, he was in the shower and once again hard as a college-aged boy at the thought of seeing her again. Nathan turned the water fully to cold to try to calm himself down, but that didn't work.

Visions of her pulling her top off, revealing dark breasts with even darker aureoles came to mind, and despite the cold water, his dick pulsed with an aching, red hot longing. He took himself in his hand and started massaging the heat of the vision out of his rock hard flesh. But as he did so, he imagined himself bending her over his desk and taking her from behind, his hand pinching her pebbled nipple as she moaned.

His hand moved swifter over the rising tide of his cum until he finally released, spraying a thick stream of semen against the shower wall and down his leg.

He breathed hard into the cold shower spray. Yes, it had been a really bad idea to ask her to come to his office in person. But he refused to let her off the hook by telling her she could mail the installment. He was the cat and she was the mouse. And at the end of day, the cat would win. He promised himself that, even as he washed the sticky evidence of his desire for Layla Matthews off his body with freezing water.

CHAPTER FOUR

INSIDE HER cozy apartment in Squirrel Hill, Layla was also cursing herself. Honor was always being touted as such a great quality to have in movies and books, but in real life, it only caused you more trouble than it was worth. For instance, if she hadn't felt compelled to pay back her father's debts along with her student loans, she might have a bigger nest egg of her own by now. And if she weren't so honorable, she definitely wouldn't be in the position of having to meet with Nathan Sinclair, a man who didn't even try to hide how much he despised her for reasons she still couldn't remember.

Moving to Pittsburgh in order to unearth the mystery of her last year here had been a gift to herself for being so good and honorable all these years. For once, she was putting herself first. She had even started saving money toward hiring a private investigator. But then she'd had her run-in with Nathan Sinclair, and her honor hadn't let her back down and walk away with a simple apology for her father's deceit. Oh no, her honor demanded she not only pay him back the money her father had taken from his family, but that she also do so as quickly as humanly possible.

She sold her car and started taking the bus everywhere. She'd also picked up extra hours by signing up for the center's mobile physical therapy service, which involved visiting clients all over the city. The extra hours wouldn't have been so bad if she still had a car. But as it was, bussing everywhere meant she often didn't crawl into bed until eleven at night, only to wake up again at five am for her regular shift at the center.

Layla had never been a complainer and wouldn't have minded the lack of sleep, except for two things: one, by her calculations, she would have to work at this rate for eight more months to pay Nathan Sinclair back, and two, he kept showing up in her dreams.

She only got six hours of sleep a night, but for some reason, an embarrassing number of those hours were taken up with images of the man she disliked most in the world doing things to her, in a large window seat of all places…sexual things, so graphic in nature she'd often wake up from them with a hot face and an aching leftover desire between her legs.

The morning of her check appointment with Nathan Sinclair had been no different. She woke up from a scorching hot dream, dripping wet, and with no time to pull out her vibrator, because it had taken her braying alarm clock fifteen minutes to actually break into her sex dream and wake her up.

"Girl, please take a day off," Peggy, the grandmotherly receptionist at the St. Mary's Physical Therapy Center said when Layla dragged into work that morning. "I'm getting tired just looking at you."

Layla tried to rub some of the sticky sleepiness out her eyes. "I'll be fine after a cup of coffee. A really large one."

"You know what's even better than coffee, I hear." Peggy leaned in and whispered like it was a state secret, "Sleep."

Layla gave her a tired smile. "I'm fine, Miss Peggy. But I really appreciate your concern. You're kind to fuss over me."

"You know what's even better than an old black lady fussing over you?" This time Peggy cupped a hand

23

around her mouth to whisper even louder, "A good-looking man fussing under you."

Layla burst out laughing. "Peggy, you need to stop."

"No, you need to stop. Literally. Go find yourself a nice man and start spending your weekends with him as opposed to all these busted up people."

Layla waved her off and continued into the center after a little more small talk. She wished she had the time and energy to date. She could use some non medically-mandated company.

Growing up, she dreamed of meeting a nice guy and starting a family. But first there had been all the physical therapy after the fall that had not only robbed her of her memory, but also broken just about every bone in her body outside of her spinal cord. Then she'd gone back to school and managed to get both her bachelor's and PT masters in five years, after which she'd worked hard to pay back her student loans in record time. The next thing she knew, she was twenty-eight, and had never had a real boyfriend to speak of—that she remembered. Obviously, she'd become desperate if she was dreaming about Nathan Sinclair every night. He just might have been the most arrogant, horrible man she had ever met—

This last thought stopped her in her tracks. What if the dream wasn't a fantasy, she wondered, but a memory of something that had actually happened? Her father had once mentioned "her boyfriend in Pittsburgh" who hadn't wanted her after she fell, who hadn't even visited her at the hospital. She could see someone like Nathan Sinclair pulling a cruel move like that. And that would also explain why she had been at his family's mansion when she'd fallen.

So far, finding out anything about her accident had been like pulling teeth. The Pittsburgh hospital had transferred her records to the hospital in New Orleans. And the hospital in New Orleans wanted a large check and either an in-person signature or a notarized document to prove she was who she said she was in order to release them to her. Meanwhile a media search at the central library hadn't turned up so much as a mention of her fall, even though it happened at such a high profile location.

The more she tried to find answers, the more she realized she was dealing with a very powerful family. They had not only paid her father off, but had also buried the story so deep, if she wanted answers, she'd have to go through Nathan to get them. Nathan who really didn't like her for reasons still unknown.

On her lunch break, she googled him to see if he had also gone to Carnegie Mellon. But his online biography said he'd gone to Yale for both his bachelor's and master's after a few gap years spent in Pittsburgh.

Again, she couldn't see how their paths would have ever crossed. She pushed back from the computer with the now familiar feeling of frustration. Why did this have to be so hard? It would have made it much easier if Nathan Sinclair had answered her questions as opposed to just glaring at her the entire time she was in his office for some crime she couldn't remember committing.

Still, her instincts were telling her that she needed to apologize to him. For what? She had no idea. But part of her deep need to pay him back stemmed from a vague guilt that had been clawing at her stomach ever since he said he didn't like her for reasons other than her father's blackmail scheme.

Maybe, she thought, she should dial up her usual niceness a notch or two when she saw him next. You can catch more flies with honey, as the old proverb said. But Nathan Sinclair wasn't like most of the other human beings she had come in contact with since her accident. He didn't exactly exude sweetness or even seem to appreciate that quality in others. Look at the way he surrounded himself with black and grey furniture and walls of hard tinted glass. Even his assistant was a block of ice. Layla supposed one would have to be to work with Nathan Sinclair day in and day out.

No, being as nice as possible would definitely not work with that man.

"Do you know anything about Nathan Sinclair?" she asked Carol, one of her co-workers, a tough physical therapist who often played bad cop to her good cop with the more difficult patients. Carol had been born and raised in "The Burgh" as the locals called it. And though Layla had only been living in the city for a few months, she had already noticed how small-town it could be. Everybody who had been born there seemed to know a little something about everybody else who had grown up there. So she figured it couldn't hurt to ask.

That afternoon they were on therapy pool duty, calling out exercises to the ten senior citizens recovering from various surgeries with aquatic movement.

"Nathan Sinclair, the rich steel guy?" Carol asked, frowning.

"Yeah, him."

Carol shrugged. "Not much. He's rich, hot as hell. But I think he only dates, like, blond super models.

People keep wondering when he'll ever settle down."

Layla could have guessed he was a playboy who didn't want to settle down just by looking at him, so she pressed for more information. "Do you know if he ever went to Carnegie Mellon? Maybe he was there for a semester and dropped out?"

Carol's forehead crinkled, "No, if he'd gone to a Pittsburgh school, we'd all know it. You know how we like to represent. But there's some other weird factoid about him that I'm trying to remember—" She broke off to yell at a senior citizen leaning against the far wall. "No slacking, Mrs. Peterson! That hip isn't going to recover by itself."

After Mrs. Peterson was back in line, doing flutter kicks with the rest of the patients, Layla said, "Good job, Mrs. Peterson. Way to come back!"

That's when Carol snapped her fingers. "Oh, wait. He didn't go to Carnegie Mellon. But you know what, his brother Andrew did."

By the time she got off work, the tired fog that had been dogging Layla all day had disappeared. His brother had gone to Carnegie Mellon, too. Finally, a break in the case, she thought as she made her way into the employee locker room...something she could hang on to and research further. She was so excited about this new information, it took her a moment to notice something off in the locker room.

As she got closer to her own locker, she saw it no longer matched the others. Hers now had words spray-painted down the front of it in red. Words that chilled her to her very bones: "LEAVE, BITCH."

CHAPTER FIVE

EVERYONE on staff at the center was horrified by what happened, but none of them had seen anything. No patients were on the premise that shouldn't have been. According to Peggy, no one had come through the door who hadn't had an appointment. The security guard even checked the surveillance cameras, which they kept at the front and back entrances, but Peggy had been able to verify everyone who came through the door that day as either a patient or a staff member.

"Why would anybody want to do this to a sweet thing like you?" Peggy asked, She rubbed Layla's back while they watched one of the center's handymen paint over the red words.

"Maybe it was meant for somebody else and they got the wrong locker," Carol said. "I'm more inclined to believe that. I know a few of my patients would love to spray paint my locker, but everybody loves you."

"Not everybody," she said, thinking of Nathan Sinclair, which was when she remembered she had been in the process of leaving to meet him when she discovered her defaced locker.

She glanced at the wall clock. "Oh no, I was supposed to be there an hour ago."

"Be where?" Carol and Peggy asked in unison.

Layla didn't answer. Just grabbed her purse and high-tailed it out of there. Hopefully Sinclair would still be at his office, because now she was even more determined to get some real answers from him.

***

Nathan had been put in a few difficult positions with women over the course of his lifetime. He'd been semi-stalked, cursed, overly-coddled, and pursued by them. But he had never in his life been stood up by one, at least not until Layla Matthews no-showed at their five o'clock meeting. At six, he sent his assistant home. No need for her to witness his fume slow-boil into rage. And rage was definitely what it had become by the time seven rolled around.

Who did she think she was to stand him, Nathan Sinclair, up? He didn't make a habit of bragging, but he was considered by certain publications one of the most eligible bachelors in the country. Most women would kill for the opportunity to be in the same room with him, but Layla couldn't even be bothered to call to let him know she wouldn't be showing up?

"Nathan?"

He looked up to see her standing at his office door. She was dressed in purple scrubs again, but this time they were covered by a white lab coat. He blinked, wondering if she was real or a hallucination called forth from his rage.

"Hi," she said in that good girl way of hers. She edged further into his office. "I tried to call, but the front desk wouldn't put me through, because your assistant wasn't picking up. Luckily, your assistant left my name on the guest list before she left, or they wouldn't have even let me up here. I'm so sorry, I'm late. Something happened at the center. And then I had to wait for the bus. And then—"

"I don't care," he said.

Now it was her turn to blink. "What?"

"I don't care," he said. "The deal is off."

"But, I have a third of the money right here." She pulled a cashier's check out of her purse and thrust it at him. "Take it."

He stood up. "No."

"Please take it," she said, her eyes hinging on desperate. "You have no idea how hard I worked to scrimp together this payment. I need you to take it."

"If you really needed me to take it, you should have gotten here on time. I would have taken it at five. I might have even taken it at six. But now it's too late. Like I said, the deal's off."

***

"The deal's off."

More than anything Layla wanted to turn on her heel and walk out of there. Pretend she'd never met Nathan Sinclair and just go. But the huge debt nagged at her. "I pay back my debts. My father used me to take this money from you, and I can't just let that lie. That's not who I am."

"How do you know?" he asked.

"What?"

"How do you know?" he repeated, surveying her under his icy grey gaze from behind his desk. "For all you know, you were the kind of person who would be okay with taking something from me and never paying me back for it."

Layla might have been tired and seriously shaken from the locker incident, but she'd have to be in a coma not to read between those lines. "Are you insinuating I took something from you? If so, tell me, and I'll do my best to give it back."

He stared at her for a few angry beats. Then he rolled down the sleeves of his light blue shirt and fastened them before jamming his arm through his suit jacket's sleeves.

"What are you doing?" Layla asked.

"Leaving," he answered. He grabbed the leather messenger bag he carried in lieu of an old-fashioned briefcase and came around the desk. "Like I said. You're late. The deal is off."

"Wait a minute," she said, rushing after him. "If I hurt you, I'm sorry. I didn't mean to. And if there's any way I can make it up to you, I will. But you have to tell me what I did."

She grabbed his arm to keep him from leaving. "Please, just tell me what you want from me."

The moment she touched him, he went still, stopping so abruptly Layla had to grab on to his arm with her other hand to keep from stumbling backwards.

"Don't," he said. The single word came out on a strangled breath, but the undertone of menace was clear.

"Don't what?" she asked, wondering why their conversations seemed to mostly consist of her asking him to clarify what he'd just said.

"Don't touch me."

Now Layla went very still. As a physical therapist, she'd been trained to be thoughtful of every patient's boundaries. She always announced before touching one of them. And if they asked her to stop touching them, she did so immediately.

But she couldn't do that with Nathan Sinclair. She had a feeling her ability to get answers hinged on her touching him, on not letting him go until he told her what she wanted and had every right to know.

"First question, how do we know each other?"

"Layla..." he ground out.

"Were we friends who had a falling out? Did your brother introduce us?" She paused to rally the nerve to ask her next question, but it still came out as a mere whisper. "We're we in love at some point?"

He kept his face turned toward the door, and they looked like a frozen picture of what they were: a man trying to leave and a woman trying to hold on to him. "No, we weren't in love."

"Okay," Layla said, picking up on his emphasized 'we.' "Was I in love with you and you didn't love me back? Did I chase after you? Get a little too pushy? Is that why you don't like me?"

His face turned red with fury. "Let go of me. Now."

"If you answer my questions, I'll let you go. I need to know if we were together. I keep on having these dreams where we're..." Layla searched for the appropriate words, but could only come up with, "Doing it. Is that a dream or a memory? The not knowing is driving me crazy. You're driving me crazy."

That's when he dropped the messenger bag and turned on her. "I'm driving you crazy? No, it's you. It's always been you driving me crazy."

Then, without warning, he plunged his free hand into her riot of curls and slammed his mouth down on hers.

CHAPTER SIX

LAYLA'S mind struggled as it tried to process what was happening. Nathan's lips were crushed to hers, his tongue inside her mouth, effectively silencing all of her questions. And even more surprising than his unexpected kiss was the way she responded to it. She'd immediately began kissing him back and flames of desire burned a path down her torso, engulfing her womb with a need so insistent it verged on pain.

"Please," she moaned against his lips, not quite knowing what she was begging him for. "Please…"

"No," he said, running kisses down her neck. "I'm not going to let you do this to me."

Then, to Layla's utter dismay, he pulled back from her, all but shoving her away from him when she tried to kiss him again. He shook his head and pointed at her, more angry than she'd ever seen him, which was saying something, since he'd pretty much stayed furious from the moment they'd re-met.

"I'm not doing this with you. I'm a grown man now. I can control myself."

Her clothes were still on, but Layla felt naked and ashamed, standing there under his accusing glare. She had no idea why she had responded to him like that, so brazen and completely willing to give him her body with just one kiss. Humiliation washed over her in waves, freezing her to the spot.

"Get out," he said. He pointed to the door she'd left open.

Numb to her very core, Layla gathered her purse to her chest and followed his directive, just as eager to leave the scene of their kiss as he was to have her gone.

But when she tried to rush out past him, he grabbed her arm, keeping her there. And with just that touch, a bolt of electricity passed between them again. She stood very still, waiting, just waiting to see what he would do next.

"Are you wet?" he asked her. His voice sounded more feral than human at this point.

"What?" she asked, confused.

"I won't be able to be gentle with you. If you're not ready for me right now, then you should run and never come back."

He was right. She should run. Send him the money she'd saved so far in the mail and then send the rest of the installments the same way, until her father's debt to his family was paid off. But...

"The truth is I'm dripping," she told him.

He groaned. "Layla, don't toy with me."

Along with being too honorable, Layla had always been honest to a fault. So she continued telling him the truth, despite her better instincts. "I can feel my panties sticking to me, I'm so wet for you."

This time when he turned his grey gaze on her, it was hot as opposed to cold. "You're wet. For me."

It wasn't stated as a question, but somehow Layla understood he was demanding a confirmation. "Yes, I'm wet. For you."

"For me," he said again.

"For you," she repeated, barely able to believe these words were coming out of her mouth or that she wanted him this bad.

He let her arm go and stepped back. "Show me," he said.

Even though he had let her go, the way he was looking at her now, like a hungry, angry animal, kept the electricity buzzing through her. "Show you?" she asked.

"Take off the lab coat."

She took it off, her eyes glued to his as she did so.

"And your pants."

She hesitated. Some part of her understood this would be her only chance to turn back, to lead with her brain as opposed to her throbbing womanhood. But in the end, she couldn't ignore the strange, sweet ache that had been building up ever since she'd met this infuriating man. She kicked off her lime green crocs and pulled down her scrub pants. This left her standing there in her pale blue panties, which just as she'd said, had a large, distinctive wet spot at the crotch.

***

It took every ounce of control Nathan had not to throw her on the floor and bury himself inside her. His throat clogged with lust when she revealed her bottom half, encased in cotton panties that, unlike the black lace his lovers usually wore, did nothing to hide her desire for him. Indeed, if he had still been touching her when she took off her scrub pants, this would all be over now. He'd have rutted her like an animal in a blaze of heat and need.

As it was, he had to turn away from her to keep from coming in his pants like a boy half his age. Instead, he forced himself to think about the performance he'd seen at the Pittsburgh Opera last spring, a world premiere, by an up-and-coming German composer known for being particularly dour. The opera had been so bleak, it had put him off having sex with his date that night. What had her name been? Samantha? Sandy? Sally? Just another in the string of blondes he had dated over the years in an effort to get Layla out of his system. He tried to recall the tune of the last aria, which had been delivered in the wasteland of a bombed out city.

"Nathan?" she said behind him, her voice tentative and questioning.

"Don't talk," he bit out.

Perhaps sensing the state he was in, she didn't say anything further, but he could practically hear her standing there, her sex calling out to his like a siren.

He couldn't remember ever being this hard without getting any release. It made it difficult for him to walk over to his desk and press the button on a remote control that tinted all his office windows black, so he could see out, but no one else could see in. Then he stripped off his own clothes, forcing himself to go slow. Humming that German aria in his head, as he folded his clothes and placed them on his chair.

Last in the series of things he knew he must do before fucking Layla Matthews within an inch of her life, was pull a condom out of the box he kept in his office drawer. He sometimes went on dates straight after work and found it prudent to pack one before leaving. But tonight, he was glad he kept an entire box at the office for other reasons. He already knew he'd need more than one before the night was over.

He ripped open the foil package with his teeth, and put the condom on before turning back to Layla.

Her eyes widened slightly and lingered on his penis. "I guess you want me, too," she said with a nervous laugh.

But he didn't laugh with her. The time for jokes

was over. "Take off your top."

She did what he said, but so tentatively Nathan had to draw in a mental breath. She had never known the effect she had on him. Her unstudied innocence, so intoxicating he'd found it hard not to believe he wasn't corrupting her somehow, even though she was standing in his office wet with her own need.

"For you," she had said. His cock pulsed again, as if it had a mind of its own and would pull itself into her vagina if it came down to it, whether he wanted it to or not.

Layla started to unclasp her bra, but he said, "No, let me."

He stepped up to her, letting her feel his erection against her stomach as he undid her bra. Her breasts, to his surprise, weren't as good as they had been at the age of eighteen. They were better. Bigger now, with hard nipples that begged to be suckled on. He bent his head to one and took it in his mouth, while running his thumb over the other one.

"Oh!" she said with a throaty gasp. "That feels so good. Please."

"There's that word again," he said. "Please what?"

"I don't know," she said.

"Do you want me inside of you?" He slipped two fingers into her as he asked her this, and his cock released a bit of pre-cum when she clenched around the two digits, pulling them deeper inside of her. "Obviously, you do."

He had thought he'd take her on the desk the first time. That, after all, had been what he fantasized about during his cold showers. But the reality of Layla was altogether different. He found himself wanting to kiss her, even more than he wanted to take her from behind. She was already close, he could feel it. And he wanted to see her face when she came. Wanted to be inside her when it happened.

He captured her lips in his and pressed her back into the closest set of windows. Then he lifted her up and in one deft movement, moved her panties just low enough to slip her wet opening onto his dick.

She was so tight, he nearly loss control of himself. "Layla." He said her name to keep himself from coming.

She locked her ankles behind his back, her pebbled nipples sliding up and down on his chest as she moved herself against him. "Nathan," she groaned back. "Please, please!" she keened.

That sent them both into a frenzy, moving against each other mindlessly as they both sought release. But when he felt his own climax coming, Nathan captured her face in his hand, holding her head still, with his thumb on one cheek and his four fingers on the other.

"I'm coming," he told her, his voice a harsh grunt. "Come with me. "

He yelled out, releasing into her in a white hot explosion of pent-up desire. "Come with me," he said again.

And she did, helplessly biting into his hand as she did so, her face the very picture of pleasure as she milked his dick with her climax.

"You're beautiful," he told her, when she finally came down. "So damn beautiful."

He rested his forehead against hers and whispered, "Now let's do it again. On my desk."

***

Layla had been a more-than-willing participant in sex with Nathan Sinclair, but she was still trying to figure out how all of this had happened. One moment, she was demanding answers from him, the next moment she was having the biggest orgasm of her life up against his office window.

He was still inside of her when he suggested the next position be at his desk, and she found herself, against all odds, clenching around his large cock at the mere thought of him taking her again. This version of her was so out of character she could barely look him in the eye as she said, "Okay, I'd like that. Thank you."

"Thank you," he repeated. "This sweet girl thing you do. That makes me wild. You know that don't you?"

"How could I?" she asked. "I don't remember you. All I know is the very little you've told me…and that I dream about you."

His eyes darkened, and he gripped her tighter around the waist. "Tell me about these dreams you've been having about me."

Layla cheeks heated with embarrassment, but he kept her pinned under his intense grey gaze, prodding her into a full confession. "It's always the same," she said. "We're in a window seat in a room with a bunch of books in it. You're on top me kind of. The window seat's not long enough for us to lay down, so I'm sitting halfway up, and you've got one arm braced against the wall, as you pump into me." She finally got herself to meet his gaze. "And it feels so good."

Something dark and dangerous flashed behind his eyes as she told him this story, and his cock swelled inside of her.

"I thought it was a fantasy, but it wasn't, was it? It was a memory."

The Owner of His Heart

He looked away from her with his jaw clenched. "I want you again, but I can't use the same condom," he said.

He stroked into her one more tantalizing time before pulling out and setting her back down on her now very wobbly legs. When she teetered, he caught her up in his strong arms, bringing his lips so close to hers, before stopping himself. "No, if I start kissing you, we'll be in dangerous territory again. Come over here."

Without warning, he swept off half the contents on his desk. "Bend over," he said, seemingly unconcerned about all of the expensive black and chrome objects he'd sent clattering to the floor.

Without thinking, Layla did exactly as he said, laying her face against the cool metal. Her nipples pebbled all over again when they made contact.

"Stay here," she heard him say behind her. He traced a hand down her back and she could feel his gaze lingering on the place where the curve of her hip met her behind. But all he said was "I'll be right back."

There were footsteps and the sound of another door—most likely to an inner office bathroom she hadn't noticed—closing.

Layla lay there with her eyes shut, spread out like a total hussy over Nathan Sinclair's desk. She had the rather alarming thought that she hadn't felt this happy, or this sexy and satisfied, in as long as she could remember.

But then she opened her eyes. As it turned out, Nathan hadn't swept everything off his desk. The computer was still there, and so were all of his picture frames, including one that held a photo of Nathan and a pretty blond, who had to be at least four inches taller and four sizes smaller than her. But that wasn't what made Layla suddenly snap out of her lust haze and stand up. What made her gather up all her clothes, hastily throwing them on as she ran out the door, was the fact that this picture of Nathan and the blond had obviously been taken at their wedding.

CHAPTER SEVEN

INSIDE his private office bathroom Nathan got rid of the condom and did his best to ignore his cock, which was painfully erect and practically screaming at him to go back out there to the delectable woman bent over his desk. He forced himself to splash some water on his face first. He had to calm down, he told himself, keep himself disengaged. He could have sex with Layla Matthews, but he couldn't let her in like the last time.

This short trip to the bathroom, reminded him of the first and only double date he'd gone on with Andrew and Layla about three months after she and his brother officially started dating. Andrew had invited him to the Sinclair mansion's game room for a round of pool and presented the double date as his idea, but it had only taken a few pointed questions on Nathan's part to get to the real scheme.

"Layla thinks we should have a better relationship," Andrew confessed. "She's an only child and she doesn't understand why we're not closer."

Nathan moved to the right side of the table to line up his shot. "And you do whatever Layla tells you to do, right?"

Andrew's fingers tightened around his stick. "She's had a hard life, and she doesn't ask for much. I figured I could do this one thing for her."

Nathan took his shot, but just missed sinking the green ball into a corner pocket. "And I'm sure the fact that you're fucking her has nothing to do with all this altruism."

Jealousy curdled in Nathan's stomach at the thought of Andrew having access to something he wanted, something he wanted bad. His masturbation fantasies had been fully taken over by the few encounters he'd had with Layla, mostly glimpses and short conversations, before Andrew came down to collect her for their dates.

But when he looked to his brother for his response, he noticed Andrew just stood there, his demeanor stiff, which is how he acted when he was embarrassed.

Nathan stood up straight with the realization: "You haven't had sex with her yet."

Obviously agitated, Andrew set about lining up his own shot. "She's not ready."

"She's a ripe college freshman. How much more ready can she be? I go through at least two of those a month."

"Not that it's any of your business, but she's a virgin. I don't want our first time together to be painful or uncomfortable for her, so I'm letting her set the pace." He took his shot, but it only sent the ball he was aiming for bouncing off two walls before it came to a meek stop just a few inches away from a corner pocket.

This left the table open for an easy shot from Nathan, and he took it without hesitation. "Man, you're whipped," he said to his brother. "If it were me, I already would have tapped that so hard."

He lined up his next shot, trying to ignore the thrill of possessive joy that lit up in his heart. Just because Layla and Andrew hadn't had sex yet, didn't mean he was any closer to making his fantasies come true with her. His thoughts darkened again. A girl like Layla would definitely want to give her virginity to a guy like Andrew. He still didn't stand a chance with her.

He sank the last ball into the right side pocket,

effectively winning the game.

Andrew huffed and put his stick away as if he were glad this farce of brotherly bonding were over. "Like I said, Layla doesn't ask me for much. Can you just play along and not be an asshole? For once."

Nathan had agreed to the double date, but only because he didn't like this longing for someone he couldn't have. Maybe, he told himself, spending more than five minutes in her company would finally kill his crazy lust for her.

He showed up to the date slightly tipsy, forty-five minutes late, with not one, but two dates in tow, his girlfriend of the moment and one of her friends, a pretty co-ed who she'd assured him would be open to a threesome later that night.

"How's it going," he asked them as he and his two dates settled in the booth. He peered at their dishes over his sunglasses. "I see you ordered without us."

Layla moved closer to Andrew, rubbing his back in a pre-emptive bid to get him to stay calm. Nathan noticed her affectionate gesture, and felt his jealousy spike once again, even though, unlike Andrew, he was sitting next to two women who were actually willing to have sex with him.

"You're late," Andrew said, between gritted teeth. "We assumed you weren't coming. And could you take off the sunglasses? It's dark outside."

Nathan's answer to this was to slide them further up his nose and say, "I've got to take a piss."

He climbed out of the booth. "Get whatever you girls want and a cheeseburger for me."

"Okay," his girlfriend of the moment agreed with a giggle.

He'd congratulated himself on finding yet another

way to ruffle his straight-laced brother's feathers in the bathroom. But when he came out, the co-ed had left and now only this month's girlfriend was sitting on his side of the booth, looking uncomfortable and somber.

"What's going on?" he asked her as he sat down.

Before she could answer, Layla covered her hand with hers and said, "Michelle has an essay due tomorrow, so she decided to cut out. I told her grades were more important than whatever she had planned with you two tonight. She's on scholarship you know, so she really can't afford to waste her time on..." She took a significant pause. "...people who might not have her best interests at heart."

Nathan glanced at Andrew, who was slouched back in the booth and smirking at him. "That's cool," he said, refusing to blow up like Andrew obviously wanted him to. He took off his sunglasses and leaned toward Layla. "Maybe you can take her place."

"Hey," Andrew said, sitting up. "Don't talk to her like that."

Again Layla rubbed his back, soothing him with just the right touch. "It's okay, I can take care of myself." She turned her eyes back to his girlfriend. "No, I prefer to engage with people who actually care about me, so I'll have to pass. Jessica, I think we have that in common, right? It's better to be with someone who cares even a little about you than with someone who's just using you for sex or who makes you feel like less of a human being. Right?"

Jessica nodded and said in a voice so soft he could barely hear her, "Right."

"Oh, come on," Nathan said.

This time Layla pinned Nathan with a look of blazing fury that took him by surprise. "No, *you* come on. Jessica is smart and generous. She deserves better. Do you care about her? Even a little?"

Jessica also turned toward him, waiting for his answer. And a thoroughly unfamiliar feeling assailed him: Guilt. "I don't want to have this conversation," he said, refusing to meet Jessica's eyes.

Layla turned back to Jessica. "Do you care about Nathan?"

"I do," Jessica said. "A lot."

"Then, Nathan, you owe it to Jessica to tell her how you feel."

"I don't owe her anything. You're the one who started this conversation."

But then the normally up-for-anything Jessica surprised him by saying, "You can't even say you care about me a little?"

He made a few calculations and decided to just go with the truth. "No, I can't really say that. You're a fun girl, but—"

She slapped across the face. "You're an asshole, Nathan Sinclair. Let me out." She pushed at him until he slid out of the booth, allowing her to slide out, too.

But before she left in a huff, she stopped long enough to say, "Thanks, Layla. It was great meeting you."

"You, too," Layla said.

They all watched her stomp out of the restaurant. The waiter chose that moment to come over with three plates of food.

"Oh, here's your cheeseburger," Layla said.

Nathan plopped back down on his now empty side of the booth. "I hate you," he said to Layla.

She grinned. "Hate's such a strong word. Eat your cheeseburger."

Both she and his brother were obviously trying very hard not to laugh.

"I'm not hungry," Nathan said.

"Apparently Michelle and Jessica weren't either. Look at all this food they left behind. If I were Jessica, I would have at least asked for a to-go bag before slapping you and storming out."

Andrew lost his battle not to laugh, letting go of his mirth with a huge splutter of air. That set Layla off. She giggled leaning her head again Andrew's shoulder. And though Nathan wanted to stay angry at the both of them, he felt a strange bubble of humor crawling up his chest, and before he knew it, he was laughing too, just as amused by what had happened as Layla and Andrew.

The three of them ended up staying at the diner until one in the morning, talking about everything from current television to their classes at Carnegie Mellon to Nathan's own future plans.

That was the conversation that convinced Nathan to stop partying and start applying to colleges. It was also the conversation that escalated his feelings for Layla from lust to love. But Layla's original plan to bring the brothers closer had failed. By the time he and Andrew made it home, after dropping off Layla at her dorm building, Nathan disliked his brother even more. Not because of their many differences, but simply because he had Layla and Nathan did not. And at that point, there was nothing Nathan wanted more than to have Layla for himself.

Nathan snapped out of the memory, arriving back in his inner office bathroom. The object of his long ago obsession was now in his office and waiting for him in a most tantalizing position. He threw one more handful of water in his face, and imagined what he'd do to her next. He wanted to taste her this time, feast on her until she keened his name and begged him to do whatever he wanted to her.

But when he walked into his office, he found it empty. Both Layla and her clothes had disappeared, leaving nothing behind but the lingering smell of the sex they'd just had and Nathan's complete and utter fury.

CHAPTER EIGHT

THREE days after unwittingly having sex with a married man in his office and two back-to-back remote physical therapy appointments on the other side of town, the 61C bus dropped Layla off on Murray Avenue. She lived about a fifteen-minute walk away from the bus stop and she usually relished the time it took her to get home. Squirrel Hill was a clean and peaceful neighborhood, populated mostly with Orthodox Jewish families and students from two nearby colleges. She felt safe there, even when walking home in the dark.

But that night the eight-block walk was a miserable slog. The summer night air felt hot and sticky on her skin, and she couldn't help but think of the last time she had been hot and sticky, in Nathan Sinclair's office with her back pressed up to one of his cold windows. An embarrassing wave of lust washed over her as she remembered what she had done. Embarrassing because she'd prefer to feel nothing but guilt where Nathan Sinclair was concerned. But when she thought about the way his chest had rubbed against her breasts as he pounded into her creaming slit, her breasts betrayed her better intentions by swelling underneath her scrubs.

What was wrong with her? The man had a wife for goodness sake. And no matter how wanton she had acted in his office, she knew she never would have had sex with him if she had known he was married. The sex had been good—better than good. Okay, it was maybe the best sex she'd ever had in her entire life. But it wasn't good enough for her to abandon her general principles.

As she got closer to her apartment building, she noticed a low slung Maserati, parked about two doors down from where she lived. She wondered who the ostentatious car belonged to. It didn't look like the kind of vehicle a college kid would drive, though she was aware a few of them had mommies and daddies who could afford to give their darlings a car that cost that much. Her thoughts drifted to Nathan Sinclair yet again. Yeah, this seemed exactly like the kind of car someone like him would drive.

Then as if her thoughts had conjured him out of thin air, his voice said, "It's about time you got here. I thought I made it clear to you on Friday, I don't like to be kept waiting."

She'd been so busy wondering about the car she hadn't noticed its probable owner, Nathan Sinclair. He seemed so out of place in his designer suit, sitting on the steps of her humble two-floor apartment building, holding a large brown envelope, that she nearly laughed. But then she remembered he was a low down cheating scoundrel and the smile died on her lips.

She decided to not to give him the dignity of a response and tried to rush past without speaking.

But he came to his feet and his free hand snaked out to catch her arm before she could get past him. "Where do you think you're going?"

That electricity zapped her again when he took hold of her arm, but this time, Layla ignored it, picturing his lovely blond wife instead.

"Inside to my apartment," she answered. "I've had a long day and I'm really tired."

"I don't care," he said. "I think you owe me an explanation for your disappearing act."

She squared her shoulders and glared at him. "The only person I owe an explanation is your wife."

He screwed up his face. "I don't have a wife."

Layla's mouth dropped open in offended surprise. The gall of him. "Where do you get off doing it with me then lying about being married?"

"I'm not married."

"I saw your wedding picture on your desk. It was at eye-level." She yanked her arm back from him. "Do not lie to me."

The look on his face switched from angry to bemused. "You really don't remember anything about me, do you?" he said. "That picture on my desk was from my brother's wedding."

Layla blinked, now confused herself. "No, he looked exactly like you."

"Yes, because we're identical twins. But you always used to say the only thing we had in common was our faces. Here I'll show you."

He pulled out his smartphone and tapped on it with his thumbs until he found what he was looking for. Then he held it up to show her a picture of him standing with a man that looked just like him. They were both dressed in tuxedoes, but the man standing beside Nathan had a much more conservative haircut. Now he was what Layla expected a CEO to look like.

She covered her mouth. "Oh."

"'Oh,'" he repeated. "I came out of my bathroom. You were gone without a trace. And then this morning I get a FedEx package with a check and no explanation for your disappearance whatsoever. And 'Oh,' is all you have to say?"

Layla folded and unfolded her arms. "I'm not sure what else I should say. I mean, yeah, I made a mistake.

But maybe it was for the greater good, because I hate to point this out, but having sex with you probably wasn't one of my brightest ideas." She ticked it off on her fingers. "You're insulting, you're aggravating, and you don't seem to like me very much. I usually prefer to engage with people who actually care about me."

The shadow of a smile passed over his lips.

"What?" she said.

"Nothing, it's just that you said something similar back when we knew each other before."

"Care to fill me in on that?"

He actually seemed to think about it before saying, "No, I don't think so."

She threw up her hands. "Whatever. I'm done with this. The next installment will come in the mail." She walked up the rest of the stairs to the front door.

"I told you, the deal is off," he said behind her.

She turned on him with vicious determination. "Listen, rich boy. I sold my car to pay you back that money. I have been working my fingers to the bone to pay you back that money. I don't care what you do with the checks, but I'm going to keep on sending them to you until I've paid off this godforsaken debt. So the deal is not off."

That declared, she pulled out her house key, but before she could get it into the lock, he grabbed her hand. "That deal is off the table, but I have a new one for you. A much easier one."

He held up the brown envelope. "Do you want to go inside to talk about it?"

"No," she said. An image of him doing what he did to her last night, but this time on a bed, flashed through her mind. The truth was she didn't trust herself to keep her defenses up if she let him inside her apartment.

"You can explain it to me here."

"Fine," he said, handing her the envelope. "I don't want you here, and I'm willing to pay to make that a reality. This contract states that you'll leave the state within two months of its execution. In return, the money you owe my family will be considered null and void. We'll also provide you with a generous moving stipend and assist you in finding a job in another city of your choosing."

Layla's mouth dropped open again as she flipped through the contract. "Anywhere of my choosing?" she said.

"Anywhere but Pennsylvania."

She looked at the contract then back up at him in stunned disbelief. "Seriously, what did I do to you?"

"There's no reason for you to stay here," he said in lieu of answering her question. "You don't have any ties to the community, and you haven't been through a Pittsburgh winter yet, but trust me, I'm doing you a favor. It's cold. And grey."

Kind of like you, she thought as she continued to scan the contract, which was exactly what he'd said, a deal contingent upon her leaving the city and not coming back for a specified period of seventy years. "I can't leave," she said. "Not until I know why you want me gone so bad."

"I don't want to live in the same city as you, and I'm very rich, so I can make that happen. That's all you need to know. Also, this deal is only on the table for twenty-four hours, so you'll need to make your decision sooner than later."

"I don't need twenty-four hours to make this decision." Layla put the contract back in its brown envelope, and held it out to him. "Sorry, but I can't sign this."

"You can," he said.

"No, I came to Pittsburgh for answers. You obviously have those answers. So if you really want me to leave, give them to me. Otherwise, take your draconian contract and go home, please. Like I've said, I've had a really long day."

He just stood there, jaw clenched, refusing to take the contract back from her. So she dropped the brown envelope on the ground and walked away.

***

Nathan watched her go, fighting the temptation to run after her. Part of him was angry she hadn't accepted the terms of his contract, another part of him wanted her to invite him in to finish what they'd started on Friday, and a smaller part of him felt vindicated. She could act as sweet and innocent as she wanted, but the Layla he'd known was still in there.

At that moment he wanted to push his hands up under her scrubs, to remove them himself this time while worshipping every curve with kisses, including the one in between her legs. But he was Nathan Sinclair. He didn't and shouldn't have to chase after women. Instead of following her inside, he picked up the contract and started back down the steps towards his car.

Still, he couldn't resist one last look over his shoulder as he did so. However, what he saw through her apartment building's glass doors stopped him in his tracks and made him turn back towards the building. On the other side of the lobby, he could see Layla standing outside her apartment door, both hands over her mouth as if she were trying to keep from screaming. Her eyes were wild with horror.

And as he came back up the steps, he saw why. Spray-painted in large red letters down the entire length of her apartment door was the word "LEAVE."

CHAPTER NINE

"LAYLA!"

Someone was calling her name. Layla tried to answer, but she could not tear her eyes away from her apartment door, which seemed to be screaming the word written on it: "LEAVE!"

"Layla!" the voice said again. But Layla still couldn't look away.

The voice got closer. "Layla. *Layla*, speak to me." A pair of hands grabbed her around the shoulders and turned her around. "Hey, look at me."

Her shoulders turned, but her neck strained to keep her eyes on the door.

"Look at me, Layla. Come on." The owner of the voice palmed her face and made her look at him.

She blinked when she saw it was Nathan. "How did you get in here?" she asked.

"One of your neighbors heard me pounding on the door."

She looked over his shoulder to see several doors stood open in the hallway and quite a few of her neighbors had come out of their apartments. A wave of embarrassment, tiredness, and confusion washed over her. It felt like her insides were crumbling into her stomach.

"Did you do this?" she asked him.

His eyes widened. "What?"

She shoved against his chest. "Did *you* do this? Were you the one behind my locker, too? You want me gone that bad?"

"No, Layla, I didn't do this." He bit the words out, like she had insulted him with her suggestion, even though he'd been trying to contractually obligate her to do exactly what the door demanded just that a few minutes ago. "I'm not married and I would never do something like this to you. Now could you stop accusing me of crimes I didn't commit and come here?"

He held out his arms to her. And Layla, too tired to question what was happening, all but fell into them, hot tears spilling down her cheeks.

He held her tight. "I didn't do this," he said into her ear. "But I'm going to damn well find out who did."

***

Less than an hour later, Nathan discovered this was actually the second time someone had left her an angry, spray-painted message. He sat next to Layla on the tiny couch in her ridiculously spare apartment while she answered questions from the two officers who had been sent to take down a report of the crime. The two officers were at least twenty years apart in age, and complete opposites. The older one was short and balding with sagging jowls, while the younger one was tall and Latino with sharp cheekbones and dark brown eyes that kept wandering back to Layla whenever he thought she wasn't looking.

Nathan didn't particularly care for either policeman, but he really didn't like the younger one.

"So you don't have any idea who might have done this?" the older cop asked. "You don't have any enemies? Any disgruntled patients?"

"No, I get along with all of my patients. And I don't have any enemies" Layla looked over at him. "None that I know of at least."

"Why are you looking at him?" the Latino officer asked.

Nathan rolled his eyes. "Because she thinks I might know something about this incident that she doesn't. But I don't."

The older cop looked between the two of them. "She might be on to something, there, Mr. Sinclair. Are there any ex-girlfriends lurking around who might have it out for your new one?"

"We're not—" Layla started.

But Nathan cut her off with a simple, "No. I don't do ex-girlfriends."

"What does than mean?" the younger cop asked.

"I don't stay with anyone long enough for it to be considered a relationship." Before the younger cop could ask a follow-up question, Nathan lobbed one of his own. "Why wasn't a detective sent to take her report? She's been threatened twice now. Shouldn't we have someone with actual investigative skills on the case?"

The younger cop's back went up when he said this, but the older cop just answered, "I'm sorry we don't meet your standards, Mr. Sinclair."

Layla laid a hand on his arm. "Nathan, don't be rude," she said. "I'm sorry, officers. He's just a little upset. We both are, but I'm really grateful you came out. And I wish I had more for you to go on."

She smiled at them, and the younger one relaxed his stance. As always with Layla, Nathan wondered if she knew the effect she had on men, or if she just wielded that wide smile of hers with unthinking abandon.

"We know this is hard for you. Here's my card," the younger cop said. He gave her a smile, one which probably came off to Layla, who liked to believe the best of everybody, as gentle, but which Nathan could clearly see for the flirtation it was. And as if to confirm his suspicions, the cop said, "Maybe we can swing by here tomorrow just to make sure everything is okay."

Nathan stood up and took the card before Layla could. He drew himself up to his full six feet, three inches, which put him at a couple inches taller than the younger cop. "That won't be necessary. Layla's coming home with me. I don't think it's a good idea for her to stay in this apartment alone."

"There wasn't any breaking and entering," the young cop said. "She'll probably be fine."

Hot anger burned inside his chest at the thought of this man using this crime as an excuse to romance Layla.

"Probably isn't good enough for me," Nathan said. And much to his surprise, he realized it wasn't. Sure he wanted her gone from Pittsburgh, but he wanted her to leave in one piece. "I'll see you two out now."

***

Layla's first thought had been to reject Nathan's offer to spend the night at his place. But she really didn't want to stay in her apartment, at least not until the door had been repainted. And the landlord had already come by and said it would take at least a couple of days for that. Actually, at first he had said a couple of weeks, but before Layla could stop him, Nathan bullied him into getting it repainted within forty-eight hours.

Nathan Sinclair, she thought to herself, seemed to have a gift for pressuring others to get his way. And

Layla again wondered what could have possibly gone down between them back in the day. Was he the Pittsburgh boyfriend her father had mentioned, and if so, what had she done to make him want her out of his life so badly?

She watched him at the door, instructing the two police officers to interview her neighbors and found it hard to believe he had a twin brother, that there were two guys as gorgeous as him running around the city of Pittsburgh—

Wait, the brother! It suddenly occurred to her that if she wanted information about what happened during the year she'd lost, there might be one more path open to her. According to Nathan, she'd once said he and his brother only had looks in common. Maybe that meant his brother was nicer than him. Maybe he'd be open to answering her questions. She had to find him. In fact, the longer she thought about it, the more it seemed finding Andrew Sinclair was the only answer to her current set of problems.

"Do you want to pack an overnight bag?"

Layla looked up. Nathan stood in the open doorway, having apparently sent the police officers on their way and was now waiting for her answer.

***

To Layla's pleasant surprise, Nathan didn't live in a large house or a high rise, but in a converted warehouse loft in the South Side, near historic East Carson Street. However, that pleasant surprise didn't last long. While the red brick warehouse seemed quaint and vintage on the outside, when he slid open the heavy steel fire door, he revealed a five thousand square foot space that looked like the home version of his office. It was filled with heavy black furniture. In the open-plan kitchen, nearly every appliance, large and small, was made out of grey stainless steel, including the square knobs on the wood cabinets, which had been painted over with black lacquer. There wasn't anything in the entire place that couldn't be described as either sleek or modern down to the slate grey cork flooring.

"Wow," she said, looking around. "This is certainly…you."

But he wasn't listening, because he was too busy typing on his smartphone in the office area on the other side of the kitchen.

"The guest bathroom is over there if you need to freshen up," he said. His voice echoed slightly in the large space.

"Thanks," she called back. Layla wouldn't mind a long bath after the night she'd had. "But, um, where's the guest bed?"

He still hadn't looked up from his phone. "I don't have one."

Layla's eyes went from side to side. "You have two bathrooms, but you only have one bed?"

He shrugged. "I'm not big on entertaining guests or sharing my space."

Layla held up a hand. "So let me get this straight. You bought an obnoxiously large loft, filled it with black furniture, and only got one bed, so you wouldn't ever have to put up with anyone who wasn't here to have sex with you?"

He chuckled. "Why do you think they call it a bachelor pad?"

She started to say something smart, but then thought twice. She was here to snoop around for Andrew Sinclair's contact information, she reminded herself, not to insult him. Instead she went over to the large black wrap-around couch and said, "Thank you for having me. I appreciate it, and I don't mind sleeping on the couch at all."

Now he looked up, his cold grey eyes almost glittering in the loft's dim light. "You're not sleeping on the couch."

"Oh, I couldn't possibly let you take the couch. Really, I'm fine sleeping here. It looks like a really great couch. Soft..."

The words died in her throat, as he laid his phone down on the office desk and started walking across the large space toward her. He paused for a few seconds, but only to strip off his suit jacket and toss it onto the couch that, according to him, she wouldn't be sleeping on. There was absolutely no mistaking his intentions, and Layla once again had to tamp down opposite urges to run and stay rooted to the spot.

Rooted to the spot won out, and she ended up feeling like caught prey when he grabbed her around the waist and hauled her to him for a kiss that pushed all thoughts of sleeping on the couch out of her head.

CHAPTER TEN

THIS was not how Nathan had expected the night to go. Growing up the scion of an old money family, life experience had taught him you could make any problem go away if you threw enough money at it. He had thought he'd get Layla to sign the contract and leave on his terms before the Sinclair Ball and his brother's return to town. But instead he'd ended up spending the majority of his evening furious at whoever had spray painted "LEAVE" on her door. For the first time in his entire life, he felt compelled to protect someone other than himself.

She had looked so scared outside of that apartment door, for a few seconds he had actually wished he could be more like Andrew, a nurturer by nature, someone who knew exactly what to say and do when women got upset. Instead, he had invited her back to his place, with a somewhat vague plan to keep his hands off of her for at least twenty-four hours, even if she was sleeping in his bed. He had never been a gentleman, but he had figured he could play the part since Layla was shaken up.

But when she offered to sleep on the couch, the old anger resurfaced. It had felt like she was threatening him, insinuating if he didn't lay claim to her and let her know exactly what he wanted her next forty-eight hours in his abode to entail, then she would relegate him to friend territory.

And he was many things, but he had never been and would never be Layla Matthew's friend. So he'd kissed her, and much like the last time, it immediately sent him up in flames. His greedy desire for her burned hot and relentless inside of him, making him unable to care what she'd been through or that she had indeed looked as tired as she said she was when they had argued earlier back at her Squirrel Hill apartment.

At that moment, he needed to be inside her, needed to know she wanted him the way he wanted, had always wanted her. And she was already responding to him – moaning underneath his kiss and rubbing her breasts against his chest, so he couldn't help but want to rip off the clothes that separated him from her beautiful body.

"Please," she said again, and he groaned. Why did she have to do this to him? Make him want her like this?

He swept her up into his arms and carried her to his bed. He removed everything but his underwear as quickly as possible, but caught her hands above her head when she tried to take off her own clothes.

"No," he said, digging a hand under the elastic waistline of her scrubs and cupping her mound, which was once again covered by a thin pair of cotton panties. "This is for me. Keep your hands up here."

He let go of her then, so he could pluck off her socks and shoes, untie her pants, and pull them down himself, revealing the lower half of her body slowly, like a birthday gift.

He moved aside the crotch of the cotton panties, and she jumped when he pushed two large fingers into her opening. "You're already so wet," he said. "We're going to have to do something about this."

The lips of her soaking slit quivered around his fingers and he could feel a responding gush of cream at his words, making her even slicker than she'd been before.

He pulled his fingers out.

"No," she moaned. Her hips lifted and grinded, seeking the heat of whatever body part he was willing to give her, and he had to work hard to get his body under control and not whip his cock out and plunge into her right then.

"Sshh," he said, pulling her panties down her hips and over her knees and finally off her body all together.

He hooked one of her legs over his shoulder and kissed the inside of her thigh, before delving into her opening with his tongue.

"Oh!" Her head lolled back and she ground her hips against his face.

Her response was almost as good as her taste. He stroked his tongue further inside of her and pushed his nose against her swollen bud, determined to make her as crazy with lust as she was making him.

"Oh, I can't. It's too much." She was panting now, but he didn't stop, instead he pushed against her with his nose again, and she bucked underneath him, her hips thrashing as her head whipped back and forth in wild abandon. Then she exploded for him, tugging at his hair and coming with one large moan.

When she was done, she sagged against the pillows, but he wasn't done with her yet. He crawled up over her body, so they were face to face. "Say please again," he commanded.

He still had his underwear on, but dragged his thick erection across her still quivering pussy, so she could feel him in her afterlight. She trembled at the touch of his cloth-covered erection, lifting her hips toward it.

But he shifted, so she couldn't grind against him, and was instead forced to feel the pressure of his cock against her opening but not have any of it. Yet. "Say please," he said again.

"Please," she said. Her eyes were helpless with need.

He pulled off her top and was grateful to find a front clasp bra this time. He released her breasts and palmed the left one. "That gets you nipple play," he said, rubbing his thumb over her hard, dark nipple. "Now say please again."

"Please," she said again without any hesitation whatsoever.

He rolled away from her and a few deft moves later, had his underwear off and a condom pulled over his large, pulsing dick. But when he lay back down on top of her, he still didn't give her what she really wanted. Instead, he lodged the large knob of his penis against her opening.

Her breathing became very shallow, and she immediately let loose a series of "Please, please, please."

"Please what?" he asked her.

"Please, Nathan," she said.

"What do you want me to do to you? Tell me exactly."

"I want you," she said, frantically trying to move her hips, but he pressed harder into her, giving her even less purchase to move and even more pressure on her aching bud.

"Please put it inside of me," she said. "Please."

"Put what inside of you," he asked against her lovely neck.

"Put your penis in me."

His cock throbbed, demanding he do exactly what she'd requested *now*. But he stayed in control of himself.

"How do you want me inside of you? Missionary? From behind? Sideways?"

Her lust-filled gaze cleared for just a moment and she looked directly into his eyes. "Anyway you want me, I want you," she said.

He had been planning to play with her a little bit more, tease her until she sobbed for it, but that statement broke him. He lifted up and plunged into her, giving her all of him in one hard thrust.

She gasped as if she'd just had the wind knocked out of her, but then she began moving her hips against his, her legs squeezing him around the waist. He lifted up on one forearm and took control back from her frenzied thrusts, forcing her into a slow, rolling rhythm with him.

She felt so sweet and tight around his manhood, perfect, like she had been created to have him inside her. With Layla, it didn't feel like fucking, but like joining, like coming back to the place he most belonged.

And when she climaxed, clinging to his back and arching up against him, lips pressed together against a scream, she pulled him over the edge, too. He released with a body-wracking shudder, pressing as deeply as he could into her before collapsing on top of her.

Breathing hard, she kissed his forehead. "Thank you," she whispered.

He didn't answer, couldn't answer for fear of saying something stupid. Like I love you. The old Frank Sinatra song coursed through his head along with the thought that he had to make her sign that contract and leave town. Not only because he wanted her gone before his brother got back, but also because he didn't know how much longer he could keep himself from falling in love with her again.

CHAPTER ELEVEN

LAYLA woke up the next morning, thinking she hadn't slept this good in ages. She stretched without opening her eyes. Even her bed felt better this morning. Her sheets were silkier as if they'd magically increased their thread count by a thousand fold overnight. And she rubbed her nose into the pillow, which felt especially plump. It was like sleeping on a cloud.

Best of all, she thought, for the first time in months, she hadn't woken up in the middle of some weird sex dream involving Nathan Sinclair—

That's when it all came back to her. Her eyes flew open and she found herself in a bed covered with black sheets, one way larger than her own modest full. She sat up with a gasp. And then she saw the stainless steel alarm clock on the nightstand next to the bed. It read eight am, which meant she was supposed to be at work two hours ago.

"Oh no," she said, scrambling out of bed. She looked around for her clothes, but she couldn't find them. They weren't anywhere near the bed, and when she opened the black hamper, she found it empty.

"Looking for something?" a voice called from the other side of the loft.

She looked up to see Nathan in the kitchen, leaning up against one of the black granite counters, wearing nothing but a pair of black workout shorts and sipping coffee from a large black mug.

For a moment she became mesmerized by the view, the way his ab muscles rippled into the hard triangle of his pelvis. But then she remembered herself and said. "I'm looking for my clothes. I was supposed to be at work two hours ago."

"No you weren't. Kate called in sick for you."

"What? Who's Kate?"

"My assistant. That's who I was texting last night." He set down his coffee and walked over to her, making no pretense of his interest in her complete nakedness. The way his eyes ran over her body sent a shiver down Layla's spine.

Still she forced herself to stay focused on the business at hand. "I can't just skip work. I need the money to pay you back—seriously where are my clothes?"

"How about this," he said, coming to a stop in front of her, so close, she could feel the heat radiating off of his post-workout body. "You sign the contract and I'll give you back your clothes."

She backed away from him, thinking that the last thing she had time for was morning sex. "No, I have to get to work."

But he caught her by the shoulders and said in a reasonable tone of voice. "Your shift started two hours ago. They've probably already called in a replacement."

"Yeah, but I hate letting people down. I should..."

He lodged his hand in the space between her neck and her shoulder, stroking his thumb against her jaw. To Layla, who could sense his cloth-covered erection just a few tantalizing inches away from her naked core, it felt like he was both caressing her and keeping her there, holding her in place.

"You're not letting anyone down," he said. "You work for a business and businesses are set up to expect their employees to use the sick days they've been allotted. Take a break from being the nice girl already."

She peeped up at him. "You really don't like that

about me, do you? That I'm nice, that I take my responsibilities seriously."

"I wouldn't know about that, actually. You've always been a hell of a lot nicer to everyone but me."

"So when we were dating or whatever we used to do together, I wasn't nice to you?"

He paused, as if considering his words, before saying, "No. You weren't."

"I'm sorry about that."

"You shouldn't apologize," he said. "For all you know you might have liked being mean to me. You always seemed to take pleasure in it, anyway."

She shook her head. "I would never take pleasure in being mean to somebody else."

"Again, how would you know?"

A flare of annoyance provided her with some respite from the thick sexual tension that came with standing here naked like this. "It's not very nice to tease me about things I can't remember."

Something ticked in his jaw, and he didn't take his hand away from her neck, but he did turn his head away from her, so she couldn't see his face. "Well, you weren't very nice to me. So now we're even."

Even with his face turned away, she couldn't help but see the haunted look in his eyes, the look she somehow knew she'd put there, even if she didn't remember how or why.

Now she reached up to stroke his jaw, turning his face back to her so she could look into his tortured eyes. "I don't know who I was then, but I know who I am now, and the thought of me hurting you really upsets me. I think that's why I want to pay you back so bad, not just because I want my dad's debt off my conscience, but because I can't shake this feeling there's something I need to be making up to you."

His grey gaze became cold again, and he shifted his eyes to a point just beyond her shoulder, obviously not wanting to answer her unspoken question.

"Nathan, no one's ever made me feel the way you did last night," she said. "I don't want to fight with you anymore, I just want to make it up to you, okay?"

He still wouldn't look at her, so she pulled the hand cupping her neck down to her left breast, hoping he could feel the heart beating underneath it. "Please, let me make it up to you."

Without warning, he turned his hand over and reversed the hold so he now held the hand she'd used to cover his in a vice grip. "You want to make it up to me? Fine, come over here."

He didn't drag her, but he wasn't exactly gentle as he pulled her into the office section of the loft. The contract he offered her last night was sitting on his desk in a brown envelope. He pulled it out with one hand, then shoved a pen into her hand, the one he had taken prisoner.

"If you really want to make it up to me," he growled. "Sign the contract."

"No!" She tried to tug her hand from his, hurt that despite what had happened between them the night before, he still wanted her out of his life.

"Then you don't really want to make it up to me, so stop saying you do." He yelled this, before pushing her hand away.

"Now if you're done pretending to be Miss Sensitivity, I'm going to go finish my coffee." He started back toward the kitchen.

Layla clutched her heart, which was beating like a wild thing inside of her chest now. Hot tears were at the surface, threatening to overtake her, but at the same time, her damn sense of honor was already telling her what she should do, what she had to do if he was serious about needing this action to forgive her.

"Fine," she said, her voice wet with sorrow and anger.

He turned around.

And just so there was no mistaking her meaning, she bent down, naked as the day she was born, and started signing the contract.

There were five post-it tabs with heavy arrows on them, indicating where she should sign her name for each section. She could feel Nathan standing behind her, watching over her shoulder as she signed away her life in Pittsburgh. Finally she reached the last page and signed that one too, scribbling the date down, despite her vision, which was becoming blurry with unshed tears.

But no sooner had she finished writing out the last two numbers for the current year, did Nathan turn her into his arms. He picked her up by the waist, and set her on the edge of his office desk. "Thank you," he said. He used his thumbs to wipe away her tears. His face was so close to hers he could feel his hot breath on her face. "Thank you. Now stay with me until you have to leave in August."

"What?" She was so sad and confused, she wasn't sure if she was hearing him correctly.

But he kissed her, leaning into her so she could feel the thick erection tenting his workout shorts. "Stay here with me. Let me have you until you go. That's the second part of my deal."

Hot need burned inside of her and she returned his kisses, even as she tried to make sense of it all. "So you want me to go, but you want me to stay with you until I do."

He reached into a nearby desk drawer and pulled out a condom. "I want to get tired of you," he said, pulling down his workout shorts and slipping the condom on over his straining erection. "I want to fuck you until I don't feel this way about you anymore."

The way he said this, it sounded like he was in pain. Like Layla's mere presence hurt him. "Then wouldn't it be better if I left now, went back to my apartment and never saw you again?"

"No." His answer was vicious and hard, like the muscles that flexed in his chest and arms as he pulled her hips toward him. "Don't leave. Stay."

Then he drove into her. Layla gasped to be filled so suddenly, but it felt good, the thickness of him as he moved in and out of her.

"Say you'll stay until your move date."

"I can't think when you're inside of me." Layla collapsed her head on his shoulder. The sensations building inside her were primal. She could feel herself clenching around him, eagerly milking him into her.

"Stay," he said, his voice low and feral. "Or I'll stop."

Layla still didn't understand why he wanted her to stay with him if he was just going to make her leave in two months. But at that point she would have agreed to anything. "Okay, I'll stay. Don't stop."

"Promise me," he said. He bit into Layla's shoulder, just hard enough, walking that fine line between pleasure and pain. "I know you take your promises seriously."

She did take her promises seriously, which was why she didn't answer him, just held on tight as he stroked inside of her, hoping he'd let the matter drop.

But then he pulled all the way out, leaving her empty and aching. He took her chin in his hand, forcing her to meet his intense grey eyes. "Promise me."

She didn't want to make the promise. But her pussy throbbed for him, her pending orgasm howled for him. And she realized at that moment Nathan wasn't the only one who needed to be weaned off this crazy passion they shared.

"I promise," she whispered.

He came back to her then, re-entered her, and pumped into her so hard and fast that within minutes, she could feel the orgasm coming, like a thunderous train barreling toward her.

"Yes!" she cried out, when it hit her coursing through her womb like hot lava. "Yes!"

This time she bit his shoulder as the tide of his release pulsed through him against the walls of her vagina. He shuddered against her, coming so hard, she could feel his jaw clench against her shoulder

"O mój boże!"

They both looked up to see a little old Polish lady in a grey maid's uniform standing there. She held a paper bag filled with groceries in each hand, and the expression on her face was thoroughly scandalized.

CHAPTER TWELVE

SAY what you want about the rest of the monochromatic apartment, it could not be denied that Nathan Sinclair had a lovely bathroom. The plush grey carpet went perfectly with the massive whirlpool tub/sauna combination shower and the silver-flecked wallpaper. The square-shaped toilet had a heated seat and even opened and closed on its own, requiring almost nothing of its users. The bathroom also hosted an array of places to sit, including a black velvet divan with sharp edges that ended up being surprisingly comfortable, even if you were in the fetal position.

Two hours after locking herself inside of it, Layla decided she loved this bathroom, and she just might stay there forever.

But then she remembered she'd eventually have come out, since she'd signed a contract agreeing to leave Pittsburgh in two months.

As if to remind her of this obligation, a knock sounded on the door.

"Layla, come out," Nathan said on the other side of it.

"No, thank you," Layla answered.

"That wasn't a request."

""No, thank you anyway," Layla shifted on the couch to face the door. "By the way, what does 'oi moi boze' mean?"

Pause. "I think it means 'Oh, my God' in Polish."

She groaned, a new wave of embarrassment crashing over her as she curled back up on the divan.

"You really do need to come out. For one thing you ran into the wrong bathroom, and I'd like to use my own toilet."

Of course, he'd be less concerned with her embarrassment and more concerned with his boundaries. Layla didn't even feel bad when she answered, "No, I've talked to your toilet and it says it likes me better. Use your guest bathroom."

"Fine, I'll just tell Lucynka that she'll have to stay late because you won't let her in there to clean."

Layla cringed at the thought of putting his maid out even further than she already had. "Can't you just tell her to skip the bathroom today?"

"Yeah, I could, but I'm an asshole, so I won't."

When they weren't having mind-blowing sex, Layla really didn't like Nathan Sinclair. Really, really didn't like him. She thought about standing her ground—or in this case—his divan, but her honor reflex was already starting to sound the alarm in the back of her brain.

"Can you at least give me my scrubs?" she asked. "I can't walk out there naked."

"I have them right here. Just open the door."

She sighed, but nonetheless got up and cracked open the door.

Nathan stood there, now fully dressed in grey slacks and a black button up shirt. He must have at least used his guest bathroom to shower, then.

He held up a bag with the name of a store she didn't recognize emblazoned across the front of it.

"What's that?"

"Something to wear. Kate dropped it off. The scrubs were nice before I discovered what was under them, but now I'd prefer to see you in something else."

Really, really, really don't like him, she thought. Nonetheless, clothes were clothes. She opened the door just wide enough to snatch the bag from him and closed it again.

Kate might be as cold as her boss, but she had great taste. Layla discovered this after showering and pulling on the strapless purple sundress. It was made out of a comfortable, soft material that felt like jersey but didn't look like it, and it fit perfectly over the matching strapless lace demi-bra and panty set Kate had also included in the bag.

Layla eventually emerged from the bathroom, freshly scrubbed with her hair finger combed into a less wild version of the bedhead she'd been sporting when she ran into the bathroom. She took a deep, steadying breath, and crossed the loft to face Lucynka.

But all she found was Nathan at his desk, working on a business document.

He looked up from his computer as she approached. "Much better," he said, his eyes darkening with approval as they ran up and down her body.

She could feel her breasts swell in response to his gaze. How did he do that, she wondered. Make her want to slap him one moment, and desire him the next? Maybe this was how he handled all his women, she thought, by confusing them with hate and sex until they just gave in and agreed to whatever he wanted like she had.

"Where's Lucynka?" she asked, finding she'd rather face his maid than think too hard about the effect Nathan had on her.

"Oh, I sent her home right after you ran into the bathroom."

Layla gasped. "You told me I was keeping her from doing her job."

He smirked. "Yes, well, I had to get you out of

there somehow, didn't I?"

Layla chewed on her lip. "Did you at least apologize before you sent her away?"

He arched an eyebrow at her and leaned back in his chair. "Her apology was getting paid a day's wages without having to do a day's work."

And the switch inside her heart flipped to off again. "Money doesn't solve everything, you know. Sometimes a sincere apology is actually in order."

He stared at her blankly as if she were speaking another language.

"Fine," she said. "I'll apologize to her myself tomorrow."

"You're getting all worked up again," he said. "Layla, come here."

He patted his lap, but she stayed where she was.

"Are you going to boss me around like this for the next two months?"

He threw her a thin smile and answered. "Yes."

"Because I don't think I'm going to like it."

"Oh, you'll like it," he said.

"I mean would it kill you to say please?"

A pause of consideration on his part. "Layla, come here. Please."

Somehow, his "please" did not sound anything like a request. But he had said it, so Layla went over and sat herself down gingerly on his knee, holding her back straight and as much of her body away from him as possible.

"Look," he said. "You can be as nice as you want to Lucynka tomorrow, but until then, can Bad Layla come out to play?"

"Bad Layla," she repeated. The moniker sent a weird shiver through her. "I'm not sure if I know her."

"Oh, I think you do," he murmured. "Bad Layla was wet for me, even before I put my fingers inside her. Bad Layla plans to have a lot of fun with me over the next two months, and Bad Layla isn't afraid to touch me."

Her throat suddenly felt very dry, like a desert. "I'm not afraid to touch you," she said.

"See if you can touch me first then, without a command."

Somehow, this sounded less like an insult and more like an invitation. One she had been waiting for, without knowing she needed it.

She tentatively moved forward, allowing her thigh to rest against his cock, which she could feel become hard as soon as she made contact. But he remained still, saying nothing, only observing her. After a great deal of hesitation, she leaned forward, tilted her head, and connected her lips to his.

She waited for him to plunge his tongue into her mouth as he had before, but he didn't. He didn't even wrap his arms around her waist. He just returned her soft, closed-mouth kiss, with his arms at his sides.

So she slipped her tongue between his lips, slowly tangling it with his, her heart cheering when he let out a groan of approval.

Something brazen rose up in Layla and she palmed his dick through his pants before unzipping and unfastening them. Her hand sought him out through the folds in his briefs, and when she found what she was looking for, she guided it out, thrilling when his penis sprang to attention, ready for action, ready for her.

"These are expensive pants, aren't they?" she said, stroking him up and down. "You're always so careful about folding them. You never just toss them on the floor."

"Well, when you import your wardrobe from Europe, you become a little reluctant about tossing it on the ground."

"Hmm," she said, biting her lip. "I just wonder if you're going to be upset about your imported pants when I cream all over them."

His cock practically jumped in her hand, and that made Layla even bolder. Despite her and Nathan's many differences, she had never felt this comfortable with a man before, especially not when it came to sex. For as long as she could remember, she'd been a shy lover, feeling more awkward than anything whenever she went to bed with someone she was dating. But it felt like she could tell Nathan anything, talk as dirty as she wanted to him, and it would only make him like her that much more.

"Layla, if you keep on touching me and talking to me like that, I'm going to come right here and ruin both your dress *and* my pants."

She let go of his long, thick penis and knelt down in front of him. "Then I should probably swallow when I do this, huh?"

She took him in her mouth, running her tongue around his thick knob at the end, before she started to stroke him again, this time with her mouth.

He breathed in a sharp intake of air. "Layla," he said. "You drive me crazy."

Layla was no porn star, but she was acting like one at the moment. He tasted so good, like mint and musk, and something so undeniably male. It sent her pheromones racing, and she sucked and licked him until he came with a grunt inside her mouth at which point she swallowed every last drop of his salty release.

But afterwards, she couldn't help but notice, "You're still hard."

He ran a hand over her hair. "Yes, sometimes that happens." He looked her in the eyes. "With you."

She reached for the drawer where she knew he kept the condoms and pulled out one foil package, which she ripped open before slipping the rubber over him with quick and efficient movements.

He nodded his head at her. "You're good at that."

"Back in Dallas, I used to volunteer with a program that taught sex education to young adults. You wouldn't believe how many cucumbers I've practiced on."

Amusement lit his gaze, "So this is your final exam then?"

She shimmied out of her dress and panties, leaving them in a pool on the floor. "Exactly. Wait until you see what I have planned for the big essay question."

Without further ado, she climbed into his lap and straddled him. She took his sheathed member in her hand and guided it into her hot, slick tunnel, loving the feel of him as he stretched her, inch by inch, until she had worked her way to his balls.

"Let me know my grade when we're done," she whispered. Then she began moving on top of him.

He grasped her hips, keeping her rhythm steady, as the fire started building up again inside of both of them. "I can already tell you it's an A-plus."

***

"We can't hide in here forever," Layla said to him two days later. The sun had risen and set, but they were still in bed, having succumbed to an afternoon nap after an impromptu bout of sex after lunch.

"We're not hiding," Nathan said, his eyes still closed, though he was obviously awake now. "We're taking a nap."

Layla hesitated, but decided to go over to Nathan's side of the bed anyway and snuggle her head into his shoulder. So far she hadn't tried this with him. Nathan didn't exactly scream "likes to snuggle." But he surprised her by wrapping his arms around her and pulling her in closer to the warmth of his body, as if he had been waiting for her to come to him all along.

"Go back to sleep," he murmured against her forehead.

"I can't. I'm hungry for something other than cold cuts."

"We'll order takeout tonight."

"And I should go check on my apartment. It's been forty-eight hours."

"Kate stopped by this morning, and she said the door's been fixed."

She laid a hand on his chest. "Could you please stop asking your assistant to do things that are way outside of her job description for me?"

"Her job description is doing whatever I want her to do."

"Yeah, but I'm sure she didn't go to college to do things like calling in sick for me three days in a row, bringing me new clothes everyday that I don't even get to really use, because you're so frisky, and now checking on my apartment."

"I tell you what," he said. "If you lie here quietly, I'll give you her address and you can send her a thank you card."

Which reminded her, she still needed to get his brother's contact information. She had tried calling him at Sinclair Industries when Nathan had been in the shower the day before, but had been told he was taking a sabbatical until early September, which meant she'd need to visit him at his home. Wherever his home was.

She had tried accessing his brother's information on Nathan's laptop, but had found it set on a lock screen when she opened it. And when she had asked to use his computer to check her email, he'd logged her onto a blank guest screen that didn't provide any link to his contact list.

She had hopes for getting the information off of Nathan's smartphone, but he took the dang thing with him everywhere, even into the bathroom. No, she had to leave Nathan's loft and do some deeper research if she wanted to find his brother before her time in Pittsburgh ran out.

"I can't keep calling in sick," she said. "Also, I should start getting ready to leave."

"You don't need two months for that."

"Sure I do," she said. "I've got to hand in my notice at work."

"It's called 'two weeks notice' not two months."

"Maybe in corporate America, but I want to give them as much time as possible to find a replacement for me. Also, I need to tell my landlord I'm leaving, break my lease, and figure out where I'm moving to."

He stiffened. "Okay, you can leave in the morning. Let's talk about something else."

Layla shifted in his arms. "Nathan?"

"Hmm?"

"Why did you make me sign that contract if you don't want me to leave?"

"It's not about what I want," he answered. "It's about what I need. I need you gone."

"Why?" she asked. "Because of what I did? Whatever that was?"

"Because of what will happen if you stay."

"What will happen if I stay?"

He turned to face her then, his grey eyes so icy, her first instinct was to shrink away. But as if sensing her inclination, he cupped a hand around the back of her neck, keeping her there. "We're not going to find out," he said, his voice harder than steel.

Then he let her go, swinging his legs over the side of the bed and picked up his smartphone. "What do you want Kate to order for us? Indian or Italian?"

"Indian, please," she answered, trying to keep her voice light.

But inside she felt her resolve becoming just as hard as his voice had been a few moments ago. She might be leaving town in two months, but before she did, she would find Andrew Sinclair.

And she would get her answers.

CHAPTER THIRTEEN

LAYLA soon discovered that finding out where a rich person lived was a lot more involved than doing a simple web search. She spent a week scouring the internet during her lunch hours, before she gave up and decided to hire a private detective to investigate.

The first detective she called asked her to say her name again after she introduced herself and then to spell it. After a bit of typing, he told her he didn't have any availability until September.

"Oh, that's too bad," she said. "Could you refer me to another P.I. Someone who might be available?"

"I don't think you're going to find anybody," he said. "Summer's awful busy."

And he'd been right. Every single P.I. she'd called informed her that he or she didn't have any availability until September, even the ones who worked for agencies told her no one was available until September.

But by the sixth no, she became suspicious. She asked her co-worker Carol to call the first P.I. pretending to be a suspicious wife, and he told Carol for a small retainer, he could start working on the case as early as the following week.

"Why you snake in the grass!" Carol put him on speaker phone, and held up her cell so they could both hear. "You just told my friend you didn't have any availability until September."

"Whose your friend?" the detective asked.

"Layla Matthews," Layla said, leaning in to talk into Carol's phone. "Hi, I'm right here with Carol and wondering why you lied to me."

The detective cleared his throat. "I didn't lie to

you. I don't have any availability for you, but anybody else, I'm willing to take the case."

"What?" Carol looked like she was gearing up to cuss the unseen detective out.

But Layla just rubbed her temple. "Nathan got to you, didn't he?"

"I can't say either way. But somebody with a lot of money let it be known he or she is willing to pay any detective in Pittsburgh you call a substantial fee to turn down your case, no questions asked."

"What?!" Carol nearly screeched.

"Wow," Layla said. "Well, thank you anyway. I'm sure you would have been very helpful if Nathan hadn't got to you first."

"Sorry, kid." The detective sounded sincere. "It's hard to turn down easy money when you live case-to-case."

"You're a slime ball," Carol informed him, pointing at the cell phone.

"I totally understand," Layla said. "And I hope you get plenty of cases to tide you over this summer."

"So why exactly are you dating this guy again?" Carol asked after she hung up.

"We're not dating," Layla answered.

"What then, you're just living together, and spending every hour you're not here with him?"

"Yeah, it's complicated," Layla said. "Do you have any aspirin?"

She ended up taking the two Aleeve before getting on the bus to Nathan's place. Just that morning, she had thought of swinging by his job instead of heading straight to his apartment, thinking maybe they could grab some dinner. But now that idea was off the table, because she already knew the only thing they'd be doing that night was fighting. This wouldn't have been so bad, but two weeks into whatever their relationship was, Layla had surprisingly already grown out of the habit of constantly arguing with him.

To her surprise, after she'd agreed to leave Pittsburgh, they'd started getting along outside of bed, too. Growing up as she did, with a father who used sweet talk and manipulation to take advantage of people, she'd found herself oddly attracted to Nathan's straight-forwardness. With other people she was constantly on guard, to make sure she didn't say anything that would hurt their feelings or make them feel bad in any way. But with Nathan, she could say anything she darn well pleased, because he had no trouble doing the same. This made him shockingly easy to talk to.

They'd discussed their childhoods, their adult lives, their hopes and dreams. She'd confessed to him about how lonely it had been growing up without a mother or any siblings. And late one night, he'd told her about the "three year rebellion," which was what he called the gap years between graduating from his elite private school and his matriculation into Yale.

"At first it was about making my parents see that they couldn't control me past my eighteenth birthday, then I got bored, but I was too stubborn to admit it. I had them worried there for a while. I think they were afraid they'd raised a deadbeat. Sometimes I wonder if my father named me CEO in his will as a thank you for finally meeting their expectations."

"What made you stop being stubborn and agree to go to college?" she'd asked.

Nathan's answer to that had been to turn away from her in bed and reach over to his bedside clock.

"I'm setting the alarm for an hour earlier. I have a conference meeting with Matsuda, and I want to go over a few details with the translator before we get on the line."

That's how Layla knew that she must have somehow figured into his decision to give in to his parents and go to college. The only thing they didn't talk about was the short time that their lives had intersected. Whenever she tried to bring it up, even accidentally, Nathan either changed the subject or made it clear it was off-limits.

Still, everything else was on the table for discussion, and when you stripped away the class and professional differences, she and Nathan had a lot in common. Disappointing fathers: his had given his life to Sinclair Industries, literally—he'd had a heart attack in his office before ever really getting to know his son as an adult. They both had delayed college experiences – Nathan's due to the three-year rebellion, hers due to the fall. They also both had a fair amount of ambition.

Sinclair Industries wasn't publicly traded and had only netted domestic contracts for almost one-hundred years, but Nathan really believed he could make the company a worldwide name, especially if they landed the Japanese deal. Listening to him talk about it, Layla believed he could transform his company, too.

The night before finding out that he'd detective-blocked her, she'd told him about her secret dream of eventually starting a physical therapy center of her own while they ate dinner. "Our patients are often so traumatized when they come to us. I wish I could make it easier for them. I read about these spas in Beverly Hills that cater to people recovering from plastic surgery, and I wondered why we don't have anything like that for physical therapy. People could come in and get their PT, but it would be in a relaxing environment. If they wanted they could get a manicure/pedicure after their session, and maybe we'd even have a hair salon. It's hard to keep up with your beauty stuff when you're in recovery, but people really do feel so much better when they look good."

She had never told anyone this or even said it to herself out loud, but it honestly felt like she could tell Nathan anything without fear of judgment from him.

"That's a great idea," he told her.

"Really?" she said.

"Yes, really," he answered. "You've got a growing market, insider know-how, and a vision. Call me when you're ready to make it happen and we'll talk start-up capital."

"Oh, I couldn't take your money," she said.

"You wouldn't be taking it. I know a good idea when I hear one, and I'll fully expect a return on my investment."

The way he said this, made her believe in the idea, too. She smiled. "Okay, I just have to decide where I'm moving to, then we'll talk."

A shadow crossed over his face, just as it did whenever the subject of her leaving came up. But then it was gone, and Nathan just said, "Make sure to do that."

Yes, they'd been getting along great, which was why he was probably unpleasantly surprised when he came home from work to find her furious and fuming.

***

The only thing that had gotten Nathan through a long day of back-to-back conference calls with Japan and a few of the other international clients Andrew should have been handling, was knowing Layla would be waiting for him at the end of it.

He'd even texted her before leaving work to say he was on his way, which he never did with women he was dating. But then again, he'd never invited a woman to share his home, even for a weekend, so all of this was new territory for him.

A certain worry crept into his thoughts as he drove home. They'd been together for two weeks now, and unlike every other woman he had dated, he hadn't grown even slightly sick of her. If anything, his need for her had deepened from an angry frenzy, to a bone-deep wanting. And it made it hard to fathom her moving away in six weeks, even though he knew what would happen if he let her stay, and there was no way he was going to allow for that.

He could still remember how stupid he had been about her before. Making excuses to visit his brother on campus if he mentioned he was meeting up with Layla, inviting himself along on their movie dates, renting a house in Miami over Spring Break just so he could invite them down. He'd even started applying to colleges, so he'd have an excuse to hang out in the library while she and Andrew were in there studying.

Then came that weekend when his parents had flown to Arizona on business and Andrew had gone on a three-day hike with the Outdoor Club. It had occurred to Nathan maybe he had become good enough friends with Layla to invite her over to their family home without Andrew.

He recalled how heavy the phone's receiver had

felt in his hand as he picked it up and called Layla's dorm room.

She'd answered the phone, "Andrew?"

"No, it's Nathan," he said, feeling more awkward than any man over the age of twelve should when talking to a girl. "Andrew's out of town."

"I know," she said. "But when I saw the number on the Caller ID, I thought maybe it was him."

Nathan decided to get off the subject of Andrew. "I, um, put in my college applications like we were talking about and I got accepted into a few of them, including Carnegie Mellon and Yale."

"Oh, that's great, Nathan," she said. "I'm really happy to hear it. Is that why you called?"

"Not exactly. I'm trying to decide whether I should go to Carnegie Mellon with you guys or maybe go out-of-state. And I was wondering if you could come by the house and help me make the decision."

He held his breath. Having just made that whole excuse up, he had no idea whether she'd buy it or not.

"Really? Me?" she said. "You don't want to ask your brother?"

"I already know what he'll say. He's a CMU Tartan through and through, his blood runs plaid. CMU was his first choice and he used Pitt as a back up, but you applied to way more places, so I think you're the better consult for this."

He half-expected her to call him out. She'd applied to a few more places than Andrew, but not enough to qualify her to give him advice about where to go to college.

"Oh, I get it," she said.

He stopped breathing and braced himself, sure she'd figured out he had a crush on her. "Everybody's out of town, and you need some company."

Layla's ability to always believe the sunniest version of a story never failed to amaze him. "Yes," he said. "The house is big, and I'm not used to being here alone."

Again, he was afraid she'd call his bluff. But then she said. "Sure, I can come over. Give me thirty minutes, okay?"

His heart jumped in his chest, excited at the prospect of being in the same room with her alone. He'd had no idea back then, what he was setting in motion.

The memory of that phone call dissolved and he came back to present day. No, he couldn't let her stay in Pittsburgh, he decided, remembering what had happened the last time. But maybe he could visit her. He really did like her idea for a physical therapy spa. And if he invested, it would give him a good excuse to go to wherever she was, ostensibly to check up on his investment, but really to get his Layla fix until he no longer needed her.

He whistled as he unlocked and pushed open the loft's fire door, but when he walked inside, he found her standing there, obviously fuming. "You paid off all the detectives in the city, just so I couldn't retain their services?"

His eyes narrowed. "You tried to hire a detective?"

"Yes," she answered. "I have the right to hire someone to try to figure out what happened ten years ago. But you don't have the right to stop me from hiring a detective." He removed his suit jacket with a sigh, kissing the happy homecoming he'd imagined good-bye and going straight back into business mode. "Layla, you're assuming ethics on my part, but I don't have any, not in this situation, and especially not when it comes to you. I don't want you to know what happened during the year you lost, and I refuse to apologize for that."

"Fine." Layla said, spreading her arms. "I can find an out-of-state detective." She went over to his desk and sat down, presumably to look someone up on the computer.

"And then my detective will find your out-of-state detective and pay him off. You cannot win this game, Layla. I have too much money, and too few principles when it comes to you."

Layla turned around in his desk chair. "Wait, you have a detective you keep on retainer just to keep me from hiring my own detective?"

He smirked. "No, Layla. I hired a detective to investigate you when you first came to town, then I kept him on to try to find out who's been threatening you. The preventing you from investigating component is only one of his duties."

Layla stared at him for a few angry seconds before saying, "Okay, I'm leaving."

Now he went from smug to confused. "Where are you going?"

"Home," she said, grabbing her purse.

"Why?" he asked. He tried to ignore the way his heart sank at just the thought of sleeping in his bed without her.

"Why? Why?! Because I'm mad at you, and that's what women do when they're mad at the guy they're with. They leave. I'm sure this scenario has played out for you before."

He shook his head, still confused. "No, not really. I'm used to a more passive-aggressive fuming in silence."

"Well, I'm not that kind of woman."

He knew she wasn't. It was one of the many things he liked about her when she wasn't trying to pry open the Pandora's box of their past. "Why can't you let this go?" he asked.

"Because it's my past, almost a whole year gone. Do you have any idea what it feels like to be walking around with a missing part of your life, especially since it had nothing to do with the fall—"

She stopped, her face making it obvious she'd said more than she wanted to.

"What do you mean?" he asked.

"Nothing." She turned her head away, studying the moonlit view of the city's landscape outside of his window.

And it happened again, that tug to help her, even if it would be against his own interest to do so.

He went over to her and ran a finger down her smooth cheek. "Tell me," he said.

She kept looking out the window as she said, "I hit my head and that sent me into a coma, but..." It seemed like she struggled to get this next part out: "I didn't have any brain damage. They did all these scans and everything came back clean, which meant there was no reason I should have lost that year. Basically it's a psychological condition. It's not that I can't remember, but I don't want to for some reason.

"They sent me to a psychiatrist, and she said I should come back here to see if anything jogged my memory. But then I got a scholarship to go back to college, and it took a few years to find a job opening in Pittsburgh. Still, I'm here now, and I need to know what happened. Please just tell me."

Layla's pleading gaze tore at his heart and made him want to tell her everything. He prided himself on being a cold bastard, tried to live up to his business reputation in every way. But this woman did something to him, made him want to do the right thing, even if it meant hurting himself.

"Ask me again in six weeks," he said. "And I'll tell you everything once you're out of the state."

"Nathan, I..." she stopped, but then decided to say it anyway. "I know we don't know each other well anymore. But I care about you. If you let me out of the contract, and just tell me what happened, maybe we could—"

"Sshh." He pulled her into his arms and held her close, breathing in her earthy scent. "Six weeks. Just give me that and if you still want to know, I'll tell you. But give me the six weeks."

She drew away from him and he could see all the questions still burning in her eyes, but she clamped her lips together before saying, "Okay, six weeks."

His heart cried out at the reprieve and he kissed her hot and hard, newly desperate to be inside her, to have her in his bed.

At that point he knew there was no use denying what he'd begun to suspect ever since inviting Layla to stay with him in the first place. He had tried to fight it with anger, with hostility, with sex, but it was too late now. He had already fallen back in love with her.

CHAPTER FOURTEEN

TWO more weeks passed by in the blink of an eye. Or at least that was how it felt to Layla, considering she still hadn't managed to find even so much as an address for Andrew Sinclair. Nathan had proven to be too distracting an alternative to her amateur detective hunt. How could she make digging around in her past a priority when her present held an extremely sexy man who she'd only be able to enjoy for a few more weeks? Also, Nathan had promised he'd tell her everything after she moved, and she believed him. He might not have been the nicest man on the planet, but he struck her as someone who kept his promises.

However, just like she'd been dragging her feet about finding Andrew Sinclair, with only a month to go until her contracted eviction from Pittsburgh, she still hadn't figured out where to settle down next. Part of her wanted to move as far away from Nathan as possible, while another part of her yearned for him to let her to stay, to forget about his stupid contract, and continue on as they were, perhaps even going as far as to fall in love—

Layla pushed that thought out of her head. She couldn't let her heart nudge her in that direction. As any simple Google search would tell you, Nathan Sinclair didn't fall in love. He dated and ditched, and from what she could see, he had never had a relationship that lasted over a couple of months. Allowing herself to even think about the possibility of falling in love with him would lead to disaster. No, she decided the morning of their one-month "anniversary," she needed to start planning for life after Nathan

Sinclair, even if the thought of letting him go made her feel a bit weepy.

She bullied herself into making a to-do list for her future move on the bus ride to work. And during her fifteen minute break, she used the smartphone Nathan had gifted her with a few days ago to research Savannah, Georgia, a hip, southern city that might appreciate a business as quaint as a physical therapy spa. But a call from Nathan himself interrupted her surfing.

"Hi," she said. "What do you think about Savannah for a physical therapy spa?"

"I'd have to research the market a little further, but if we're just speculating, it sounds fine."

"Well, then how about—"

"What are you doing for lunch today?"

The abrupt change of subject didn't surprise Layla. As their time together decreased, so had Nathan's willingness to talk about her move, even though he was the one who had forced it on her. "I was just planning to grab a sandwich from the vending machine."

"How about coming downtown and having your sandwich here? I'll have Kate order something for us."

"You're inviting me to lunch?" she asked. He'd joined her in Shadyside once or twice, but had never invited her downtown.

"I'm inviting you to lunch," he said. "You know, I never did get to have you bent over my desk. I think you owe me a position."

Her cheeks heated remembering the first time they'd had sex. But then she realized, "There's no way I could get downtown on a bus and get all the way back here in time to start my shift."

"Oh, I've already taken care of that. Go to the parking lot."

"Did you send a car service again?" she asked, walking toward the lobby and out the glass doors. "My lunch hour doesn't start until one today."

"Do you see a red Mini?"

Layla found said red Mini in one of the closer parking spaces, gleaming under the August sun. It still had its dealer's plates. Her heart stopped. "You didn't…"

"I'm sick of you using that 'no car' excuse to squirm out of anything you don't want to do."

Layla ran out to look at the car, which happened to be exactly the one she had always dreamed of owning.

"I've never used not having a car as an excuse. I'd love to have lunch with you, but I can't possibly take a car from you. It's bad enough that you got me the new phone, because you said you wanted me to be accessible by email. Now you're buying me a car?" But even as she said this, her eyes ran greedily over the delectable vehicle. She'd always had a thing for Minis. "A really nice car."

"Layla, do you seriously want to fight me on this? Haven't I proven how hard I am to say no to yet? What else do I have to do?"

He made it sound like he was the aggrieved party here, and Layla was just being difficult.

"Don't be difficult," he said, echoing her thoughts in his all-business tone. "I just want to ensure I see you in a timely manner not dictated by the Pittsburgh bus schedule."

"Yeah, but how can I ever pay you back for this?" she asked, her voice small.

"Well, I do have this black-tie fundraiser for the Pittsburgh Opera next Friday. It's going to be hellishly boring, but I have to go because I'm on the board. You could come with me. Then we can call it even on the car."

Layla smiled into her phone. "I would have come with you anyway," she said. "All you had to do was ask. No car needed."

"I'll remember that next time," he said. "Kate left the keys on the front wheel."

She groaned. "Please tell me you didn't inconvenience her again for me."

"I'm hanging up on you before you convince me to triple her holiday bonus just for doing her job."

She bit her lip. "It doesn't have to be triple. I'd settle for double."

"Goodbye, Layla."

"Or at least let me pick out something really nice for her Christmas present before I leave. It's the least I could do."

"We'll talk about it when you get here. See you then."

Before she could answer he hung up, leaving Layla alone with her new car and the feeling it was just going to become harder and harder everyday not to fall in love with him.

***

A couple of hours later, Kate buzzed into Nathan's office. "Two things," she said. "Layla's on her way up."

"Great, great," he said. "Just send her straight in."

"And your brother's on line one."

Nathan paused. At the beginning of the summer, he would have jumped at the chance to harass his brother to come back to Pittsburgh. Nathan had been handling all the negotiations with Matsuda along with the other global initiatives Andrew had abandoned. But with Layla on her way up to his office, Andrew was the last person he wanted to talk to.

He sighed. "New plan: keep Layla out there with you while I deal with him."

"Yes, Mr. Sinclair." Kate signed off.

He pushed line one and said, "Andrew."

"Nathan," his brother answered. "I've given this a lot of thought, and I can't come home. Not yet. I'm going to ask Diana for a divorce, and if you don't want me to do it before the ball, then I'll just have to skip it. It's dishonorable to be in the same room with her, when I know we're only using her to host a party at this point."

"You and your honor," Nathan said, his thoughts going to Layla. "I'm sure Diana's alimony check will more than make up for all of her hostess duties."

"She's a human being with feelings," Andrew said. "Do you get that I'm about to ask her for a divorce? Our marriage has fallen apart. Why do always assume everyone can be bought off?"

Again Layla drifted into his mind. His parents hadn't approved of her and Andrew's relationship, but everyone else had. Their friends, the Sinclair servants, even strangers on the street had said they made the perfect couple. Jealousy burned through Nathan just thinking back to those days when he'd had to watch them afar, wanting what Andrew had so badly, but not being able to do anything about it.

"Fine, don't come to the ball," he told his brother. "I'll handle it and Diana, who keeps on calling me, asking if I know anything about your whereabouts. I'll let her know you're not coming home until after the ball, because you're oh-so-concerned about her feelings, which is obviously why you disappeared and haven't given her so much as a call since you did. I'm sure she'll come away from this all seeing how honorable you are."

Then, for the second time that summer, he hung up on his brother.

***

Outside Nathan's office, Layla twiddled her thumbs. She was experiencing a certain sense of déjà vu, sitting on the same couch as before, waiting for Nathan to finish up whatever business he was conducting behind closed doors.

"Do you know how long he's going to be?" Layla asked his assistant. "I only have an hour for lunch."

Kate didn't look up from her computer. "I'm sure it won't be long."

Layla sat forward on the grey couch. "By the way, I want to thank you for everything you've done since my apartment door got vandalized. I loved all the clothes you sent over, too. You have great taste. And I really appreciate you dropping off the new car. I'm already in love with it."

"No need to thank me," Kate said.

An awkward silence descended once again.

Layla said, "You must need a really interesting skill set to get a job like this. One day you're doing administrative stuff and the next you're shopping for Nathan's women friends. Plus you're on call twenty-four-seven."

"Mr. Sinclair asks very little of me outside of office hours, so I really don't mind the few occasions when he does," Kate said.

"Really? Very little? I mean all the stuff he's asked you to do for me alone, not to mention the women who came before me—that doesn't seem like very little."

"Actually it is." Kate finally looked up at her. "He's never asked me to do anything for the other women he's dated. Not so much as buying a Christmas or birthday gift. Just you."

Layla shook her head. Surely, Kate was kidding. She couldn't be the only woman Nathan had ever asked Kate to shop for. She'd thought for sure all the gifts and clothes were his usual M.O.

But before she could question Kate further, Nathan buzzed into the outer office. "I'm off my call. Send her in," he said. His voice sounded clipped.

When she walked in, she found a table already set with gourmet sandwiches, an open bottle of Perrier, and a cheese plate on one side of the office, and Nathan visibly fuming behind his desk on the other.

"Is everything okay?" she asked.

Nathan just stared into space, his jaw set tight.

"Nathan?" she said, real worry creeping in as she rounded the desk to go to him.

But then the cloud passed over his face and he said, "Bad business call. Somebody I was counting on let me down."

She stroked her hand through his soft hair. "Want to talk about it?"

He smiled, but to Layla it looked a little sad. "No, I don't."

Then, like a robot come to life, he stood up and

began to remove her clothes with rough, jerking movements. "I need you," he said.

Once she was naked, he swept the desk and bent her over it, working two thick fingers into her wet tunnel. "Open for me," he said.

Layla could feel her juices coming down, as if they were at his command. The heat building up in her was in direct contrast with the cold metal of his desk, which she rubbed her pebbled nipples on as she moaned and squirmed against his demanding hand.

Behind her, he said, "You're ready for me."

She couldn't tell if this was a statement or a question, but either way, she answered, "Yes, please, yes."

This time there were no sounds of a condom being taken out and put on. She'd started taking birth control at the beginning of their two months together, so when he entered her, there was nothing but delicious skin-on-skin contact.

One hand worked her clit and the other hand held her steady while he pumped into her faster and faster until they both came. Layla moaned as load after load of his semen flooded her, his cock pulsing in her afterlight.

Afterwards, he pulled her up from the desk and turned her around in his arms, kissing her hard as their orgasms finally receded.

"How do you do that?" he asked against her lips. "Make me want you like this? It feels like I can't get enough of you."

She could feel him growing hard again as he said this, and her own desire reignited, despite the fact that she had just come. "I was about to ask you the same thing," she said.

CHAPTER FIFTEEN

GETTING cleaned up for a black tie fundraiser turned out to be serious business. Layla had to take half a day off of work because Kate had jammed her Friday with so many beauty appointments: first, she'd gotten exfoliated and buffed from head to toe, waxed just about everywhere, with a mani/pedi to top it all off. Then she'd had to rush back to the loft to meet up with Mark and Jacob, a hair and make-up team. They'd worked on her in a whirlwind of gossip, fake eyelashes, and flat irons, which culminated with them zipping her into the light blue sheath dress Kate had picked out and guiding her to the wall of full-length mirrors in the home gym portion of the loft.

At first Layla couldn't believe the vision in the mirror was actually her. The dress hugged her curves perfectly, making her body look more like a work of art than the bag of bones she'd had to drag out of bed that morning. Though Jacob had spent an hour on her make-up, she somehow looked fresh and dewy, like she'd just thrown some lipstick on and her face was always this big-eyed and gorgeous. And her hair—in the up-do Mark had fashioned, she could have passed for a glamorous movie star from the forties. No one looking at this version of her would be able to guess she was an overworked physical therapist in real life.

"You're miracle workers," she said to Mark and Jacob.

They just laughed, and complimented her for being such a wonderful palette. Then Jacob spritzed her with expensive perfume and they left in a flurry of upkeep instructions and air kisses. Before she even had time to catch her breath, the car service buzzed to say the limo Kate had arranged was waiting for her downstairs.

But all the trouble was worth it for the look on Nathan's face when she walked into the lobby of the Pittsburgh Opera. He'd been talking to another man in a tux, but walked away from the conversation without a word of explanation as soon as he spotted her, not stopping until she was in his arms, her lips crushed beneath his.

"You look good," he said, by way of explanation when he finally released her from the kiss.

"You stole all my lipstick!" She laughed and wiped the color off his lips with her thumb. Luckily Jacob had given her an extra tube for reapplications.

He grinned. "You had it coming. Walking in here looking this good—you had to know how I would respond." He secured an arm around her waist and guided her deeper into the party. "Let's start doing the rounds, so we can get out of here in fifteen minutes."

"I spent half a day getting ready for this party. We're not going to just skip out," she said.

"Okay, half an hour."

"Two hours."

"One hour. That's my final offer."

Layla laughed again. "Fine, Nathan."

She thought she'd spend most of the party listening to Nathan talk business with his other associates, many of whom also served on the opera board, but to her surprise, he included her in every conversation, even going so far as to steer the dialogue back to topics she could discuss when it became too business-oriented.

It helped that Layla had already converted to

Pittsburgh sports fandom, able to hold forth on why the Steelers were the best football team on earth, bemoan the ever-losing Pirates, and talk passionately about how the Mario Lemieux-led Penguins had convinced her to give hockey a chance.

Nathan disagreed with her on all counts, which meant even his own friends took her side over his and were happy to help her gang up on him when he tried to argue for the Patriots, the Cardinals, and Canada's hockey teams. This started an inflamed conversation that kept them laughing, and soon other people at the party joined their circle, as if attracted by their loud arguments and sparkling back and forth.

Layla had expected a stodgy party, but she couldn't remember the last time she had laughed this much. And when Nathan called time on their hour, she groaned. "I'm having so much fun. Can't we stay a little longer? I'll give you a five-minute kiss break."

"The reason I want to leave is so I can kiss you without time limits. Besides if we leave now, we don't have to sit through the boring speech."

Layla winced. "But shouldn't we stay for the speech? I mean you are on the board. You should be more supportive."

He chuckled, "Only you would try to guilt trip me about skipping a fundraising speech."

"Just twenty more minutes," she said. "I didn't go to prom, so this is my first fancy party. Like ever."

He pulled her into his arms, folding his hands behind her waist. "You did really well tonight, Layla. Haven't you ever heard of leaving them wanting more?"

"But I'm leaving in two weeks, so even if they wanted more, I wouldn't be able to give it to them."

She had meant this as a joke, but a certain sadness

permeated the air between them as they both seemed to realized this would indeed be the last "fancy" party they ever attended together.

But then he said. "No, we can do this again. You can be my date to the Sinclair Ball in two weeks. It will be our last hurrah."

She scrambled to recapture the previous breezy mood they'd struck. "I don't know," she said. "Will it be as fancy as this event?"

He took her empty champagne flute and handed it off to a passing waiter. "Even fancier. Now do me a favor and go reapply your lipstick, so I can take it off again in the limo."

But before she could untangle herself from his arms, he kissed her again, this time a chaste buss and then another and another, as if he was looking for any excuse to give her extra kisses, even though he was the one kicking her out of town.

When he finally let her go, Layla felt a now-familiar melancholy come over her at the thought of leaving in two weeks, and true anger rose within her. Why was he making her leave? Why couldn't he just forgive her for whatever it was she'd done? Most of all, how could he not feel about her the way she was beginning to feel about him after six weeks together?

In the restroom, she reapplied her lipstick on autopilot, wondering if this was how all the women he dated felt, like they were the center of his universe and maybe had a chance at winning his love—until he got rid of them the way he was about to get rid of her. If only she could find his brother. Maybe he knew something, something she could use to convince Nathan to let her stay.

"Layla? Layla Matthews?" a voice said to the right

of her. She looked up to see a plump, red-haired woman in a black dress with a sweetheart neckline. "I thought that was you, when I saw you in the lobby, It's me, Jessica."

Layla shook her head.

"Oh, I know it's been a while, but surely you remember that night with you, me, Nathan, and Andrew. That disastrous double date." Suddenly her face fell. "You don't remember me. It's because I've gained so much weight, isn't it?"

"No, that's not it at all." Layla reached out a hand to soothe the distraught woman. "I had an accident, you see. I fell and I lost a chunk of time, my entire first year of college. Maybe we met then?"

Layla sure hoped so, because the woman looked like she was about to burst out crying.

Jessica's eyes widened. "Yes, that's when we met. Really? You lost an entire year? You're not just saying that to make me feel better?"

Layla smiled. "Well, I'm nice, but no I wouldn't fake a head injury to make you feel better."

The next thing Layla knew, Jessica had gathered her up in a hug. "Oh, you poor thing. You poor, poor thing," she said. "I can't believe something like this happened to you. You were so nice."

"I'm still here," Layla said, gently disengaging herself from the smothering hug. "No, need to refer to me in the past tense."

"Yes, you're still alive. How lucky. And I saw you kissing your college boyfriend in the lobby, so it looks like you're back together."

Layla demurred with a shy head tilt. "I wouldn't say back together. I didn't even remember him when we saw each other again three months ago, the first time since my accident. And I'm moving to Savannah in two weeks, so who knows how it will all turn out."

But Jessica shook her head, grabbing Layla's hands with emphatic fervor. "No, you two were perfect together. Everybody used to say so."

"Really?" Layla said. "Because we're pretty opposite in most regards."

"Maybe you two come from different classes, yes. But you're both such gentle souls."

"Gentle?" Layla said, because that would be the last word she'd use to describe Nathan. He didn't have a gentle bone in his body, but maybe he was a lot different back then.

Her brain seized. Could it be possible that whatever she had done had made him this way? Was that why he'd been so adamant about her leaving town?

"Though, I must say I'm surprised to see he's broken up with Diana. I mean I heard they were having problems, but I didn't know they had separated. Or are they already divorced? Heaven knows, you can push those through pretty fast if you have a tight pre-nup, which I imagine they did as much money as both their families are worth."

Then it became clear to Layla what was going on. "Oh, no, I think you're confused. I'm not here with Andrew. I'm here with Nathan."

To Layla's surprise, Jessica's face went from happy to angry, complete with narrowed eyes. "What?" she said.

"That's who I was with in college, right? On our disastrous double date?" Layla asked, though the worst feeling was starting to steal over her.

"No," Jessica said. "I was with Nathan. You were

with Andrew. From what I could tell, you and Nathan hated each other."

CHAPTER SIXTEEN

SIX weeks ago, Nathan had hoped inviting Layla to stay with him would cure him of his infatuation with her. It had done the opposite. When he first proposed her staying with him for the two months before she had to move, he'd seen himself kicking her out after two weeks, a month tops. He'd figured he'd get sick of the adult version of Layla, like he'd gotten sick of all the other women before her, no matter how beautiful they were.

But that hadn't happened. In fact, given an inch, Layla had taken a mile. She'd yet to use the guest bathroom, insisting on using his, even going so far as to force him to share it with her, on the few days when he had to get to work early for a conference call with Japan or one of the other would-be global markets. Layla might seem like a pushover to everyone else, but he had serious problems cowing her anywhere outside of his bed. He'd always burned the midnight oil, but these days he went to bed earlier, because Layla had to be up in the morning for her shift. Not only had he'd decided to double Kate's bonus at her behest, but also Lucynka's who Layla insisted was still owed something due to the one time she'd caught them having sex. He'd taken to saying thank you, at first to stave off arguments with Layla, but over the course of the summer it had become a habit.

Worse of all, he'd found himself enjoying his time with Layla for reasons outside of sex. He actually liked having her in his space, looked forward to coming home to her ever-smiling face. Before Layla he'd watched CNN and the Military Channel in the evenings, with a few episodes of *Top Gear* thrown in for fun. But over the course of the past two weeks, he'd started watching summer reruns of a few night time dramas Layla liked and had gotten caught up in the story lines himself.

It had all grown very domestic, which made her leaving that much harder. He got angry just thinking about her moving on with her life, finding another boyfriend, maybe even marrying and having children. Sometimes when they were making love, it got so intense, he'd think to himself, "You're mine, and I'm never going to let you go." And he'd feel this so deeply, he'd come before he was ready, with the primal urge to spill his seed inside her, to put his baby inside of her, even though he knew she was on birth control. And even though he also knew she'd be leaving Pittsburgh soon at his behest.

But things between them began to sour the night of the opera fundraiser. It all started when their conversation hit an awkward note just as they were about to leave the gala. He'd thought inviting her to the Sinclair Ball would fix it, and it had for a minute or two. But then she went to the bathroom and emerged over fifteen minutes later with fresh lipstick and a changed demeanor. Her smile had completely disappeared, and her gaze kept skittering all over the place, never quite landing to meet his.

"Is everything all right?" he asked, already worried that it had taken her so long in the bathroom.

She shook her head and said, "No, I just have a migraine. I took something, but it still hurts."

That night they went to sleep on opposite sides of the bed, with Layla claiming she was in too much pain to fall asleep in his arms as she normally did. And when he woke up she was gone. He found a note left on the refrigerator, explaining she needed to run a bunch of moving-related errands.

Apparently these errands took up most of the day, because she called late Saturday night to say she was exhausted from packing all day and was just going to sleep at her apartment that night.

"You can sleep over here," he said.

"I don't get a lot of sleep when I'm over there," she answered.

"I'm not an animal. I can keep my hands off of you for two nights in a row. Now three, and we might have a problem."

This had been a joke, and he expected her to laugh, but she just said, "I really don't feel like driving. I'm just going to stay here."

"I'll send a car."

"Don't. That's too expensive."

Despite having been with him for six weeks, Layla still didn't seem to grasp how rich he was, and that she didn't have to worry about how expensive things were, because he could afford it. Buying her anything continued to be a battle. One he didn't feel like waging with her at that moment.

"Okay, then, I'll come and get you."

"No, Nathan. That's so far out of your way. Seriously, it's okay. I can sleep here today and tomorrow."

"Today and tomorrow?" he said. "When did it become today *and* tomorrow?"

"Well, I figured if I got everything out of the way now, then I'd have more time to spend with you before I go. But that means I really have to concentrate on getting everything done. No distractions."

He knew she was attempting to tease him with the last line, but he couldn't laugh, because he was suddenly overcome with an unfamiliar urge to beg. He didn't want her to take two nights off from their relationship—in fact, the thought of not seeing her until Monday made him heartsick. So as always, when she made him feel things he didn't want to feel, he got angry.

"Our agreement states that you'll stay with me," he said, deliberately making his voice cold and business-like. "That means wherever I am, you're supposed to be."

A frosty silence came down the line. And just in case that hadn't been enough to convince her, he said, "You promised, Layla. I thought you always kept your promises."

More silence. Then she said, "Fine" and hung up.

He'd tried calling her back, but she didn't answer. Twenty minutes later, he was just about to grab his keys and go over to her apartment himself, when she came through the front door, already dressed in her pajamas and looking as tired as she had claimed on the phone.

"Layla," he said, happier than he wanted to be to see her.

But without even acknowledging his presence, she went to the bed, climbed in, and closed her eyes. She didn't even respond when he got into bed himself and pulled her into his arms. But she didn't push him away either, so he settled for this. A pissed off Layla, he decided, was better than no Layla at all.

He'd thought they'd talk about what happened in the morning, but when he woke up she was gone again and this time she didn't come home until after midnight, once again climbing into his bed without a word.

"Layla, I'm not going to let you do this two nights in a row," he said to her back, after getting into bed himself. "If you're angry at me, tell me. I won't put up with the silent treatment."

"What is there to say?" she asked, her back rigid. "I'm leaving in two weeks. I'm just trying to get ready for my contractually-obligated move."

He could feel resentment and anger radiating off of her, and even worse, he started to get angry at himself for forcing this move, even though he had his reasons for demanding she leave Pittsburgh altogether.

"I get that you want me when you want me, however you want me for a limited period of time, then you won't want me anymore," she said. "I get it. I do. But it makes me feel terrible inside. I'm sorry that sometimes I have a hard time acting like it doesn't. I'm not a robot, like you."

He wanted to hold her. He wanted to tell her he would never get tired of her, because at that moment, as much as he didn't want it to be true, he could feel it's truth in his heart. He wanted to tell her he loved her, had been in love with her for ten years, even when he had thought he hated her. But every word, every action he considered was a Pandora's box that couldn't and shouldn't be opened.

So instead he stayed quiet. The next day when he woke up, she hadn't disappeared like the two mornings prior. But somehow watching her get ready for work without a word was even worse. She usually played music or rattled on about her patients, the ones she was worried about, and the ones who were recovering faster than expected. For someone who was used to getting ready in solitary silence, her chatterbox ways should have been irritating, but he'd liked her stories, liked hearing about the ups and downs of her job, which was so different from his own.

But that Monday morning it felt like he was dealing with the ghost of the woman he'd come to know. And by the time he made it to work, he was furious with both her and himself.

He couldn't help but think back to ten years ago, to the night that had changed everything.

***

When Nathan had invited Layla over to the Sinclair mansion to help him choose a college, he'd only had a vague idea of what he'd do after she arrived. Yes, he wanted her in his bed, but he had no idea how to get her there. Usually, he didn't have to do any work when it came to girls. If he saw one he liked, he said "Hello," and then an appropriate amount of time later, "Where do you live?" which eventually led to sex. Sometimes he didn't even have to go this far. Girls would just throw themselves at him, making any effort on his part moot.

But Layla wasn't like other girls. Although, they'd been getting along since the double date, she'd never given any indication she thought of him as anything more than her boyfriend's twin brother. There'd been no sly looks behind Andrew's back or even a hint of mild sexual interest. And sitting with her legs crisscrossed in the library's large window seat, going over the brochures for the five schools that had accepted him for next fall, she'd actually seemed intent on helping him choose one.

"I know you just got me over here for the company," she said, after putting down the last brochure. "But I really think you should go with Yale. You're probably leaning toward Harvard because your dad went there, but I think Harvard will only exacerbate your douchebag tendencies."

He laughed. "My douchebag tendencies? Wow, tell me what you really think."

"I am," she said with a gentle pat on his knee. "Keep in mind, I didn't suggest you should go the small Ivy liberal art college route, because you might need those douchebag tendencies later, and I don't want them to beat that out of you. Yale seems like a happy medium: name recognition, but less cut-throat than Harvard. I think you could be happy there."

He grabbed the Yale packet and said, "Okay, Yale it is."

"What?" she said. "Just like that?"

"I respect your opinion."

"You're not serious," she said, even as she watched him sign the acceptance letter and a few more forms before sliding them into the return envelope.

"Completely serious," he answered. "I'm going to put this in the mail tomorrow. Thanks for the advice."

"No, thank you," she said. The giddy smile that broke out across her face just about stopped his heart. "No one's ever trusted me with such a big decision before."

And then she hugged him, enveloping him in her warmth and curves, so he could barely think, much less keep himself from saying, "I love you."

She pulled back, her face going from smiling to confused. "What did you say?"

"You're beautiful," he repeated, unable to stop

himself now that he had started. "And I'm in love with you."

Layla let him go, un-crisscrossing her legs and turning away from him. She balled her hands in her lap and stared at them, obviously trying to think of a nice way to let him down.

He, too, turned to face front, and he stared at his own hands folded in his lap as he said, "I know you belong to Andrew, but I love you, more than he does, more than anyone else ever could, and I had to tell you."

He waited for her to let him down easy. He'd never been let down easy before, but Layla seemed like the kind of girl who would be good at that: attracting the wrong kind of boy, then having to break his heart.

But when she looked up, her eyes were glistening with tears. "I think I'm in love with you, too," she whispered. "No, actually, I know I am. I've been fighting it so hard, because I didn't want to hurt Andrew, but I don't love him. I love you."

Nathan wasn't sure who reached for who, but the next thing he knew, she was in his arms and they were kissing. And it was better than anything he had daydreamed. If not for the hard sexual need burning inside of him, he could have stayed there kissing her forever. But she was rubbing her body against his, and his body was also demanding more. He barely had time to sheath himself in the condom he kept in his wallet, before he'd pushed up her skirt and entered her. Sinking into her warmth felt like a dream come true. Not until she audibly winced with a sharp intake of air did he remember her virgin status.

"Oh, shit, Layla, I'm sorry," he said, freezing inside of her. He stroked a hand over her short hair and laid his forehead against hers. "If I had remembered, I never would have—" He stopped himself there, because he didn't want to lie to her. As crazy as he was about her, nothing would have stopped him from making love to her. But now he found himself wishing he could have made her first time more romantic, or at least laid her down on a bed before mauling her.

However, she interrupted his self-castigation with a whispered, "Nathan, I love you. I'm glad you're the first. But could you please start moving again."

He happily accommodated her request, pumping into her with only slightly less abandon than before. He had never wanted anything as much as he wanted her. All thoughts of Andrew disappeared from his head and so did the rest of the world as he braced himself against the edged of the curved window seat and moved inside of her. A sweet hurt built up inside his groin, begging for him to release. But he denied himself, desperate to please her, to show her he was a better choice than Andrew in every way, even if it didn't seem so on the surface.

"I love you," he whispered, over and over again into her ear, until she finally climaxed for him.

"Nathan!" she cried, clenching around him, drawing him even further in as they both came.

Afterwards, they didn't talk about what they had done, just straightened themselves out enough to look decent when they walked through the house to the one-bedroom guest cottage he occupied behind the mansion. He led her straight to his room, and this time they took their clothes off before making love again. Nathan could still remember how happy he'd felt as he fell asleep with her wrapped up in his arms, like he could accomplish anything and everything now, just because he'd won the heart of Layla Matthews.

But the next morning he'd woken up to find her gone. At first he wondered if it had all been a dream. But no, there was his acceptance letter to Yale, sitting on his desk, packaged and waiting to go.

It occurred to him Andrew was due back that morning and Layla might have taken off rather than risk getting caught cheating on him with his twin brother.

Nathan should have felt more guilty about stealing his brother's girlfriend, but the truth was, she had always been his, from the moment he met her. To Nathan's way of thinking, his brother was partly to blame for meeting Layla first and taking something that didn't truly belong to him.

Knowing Layla, she was sitting in her dorm room at that moment trying to think of the best way to let her brother down. But Nathan already knew the best method would be to rip the band-aid off. It would be better for Nathan to tell it to his brother straight, without subjecting him to the embarrassment of Layla's profuse apologies.

So he went to the main house to do this, climbing the stairs to his brother's suite. He could see the door was open, which meant he was already back from his trip.

It occurred to Nathan at that point that maybe he shouldn't go to Yale after all. He'd rather be here with Layla at Carnegie Mellon, than a six-hour drive away in Connecticut. But Layla probably wouldn't go for it. With that misguided sense of honor she had, he could already hear her saying they shouldn't rub their relationship in Andrew's face—

That's when he saw them. Layla wrapped in

Andrew's arms as he kissed her with a passion Nathan hadn't even known his staid brother possessed.

First it felt like a punch in the gut. Then his heart cracked into a thousand pieces, leaving nothing behind but a black ball bitterness and hate.

As if sensing him his presence in the doorway, they both looked up.

"Nathan," Layla said.

But he didn't stay. He refused to stand there while she let him down easy, explaining why she'd obviously chosen his brother over him. He walked away, ignoring Layla calling his name. Why had she told him she loved him? Maybe it wouldn't have hurt so bad if she hadn't lied to him, but he had believed her, and left himself unprotected. It felt like Layla had plunged a knife into his heart and he had just walked right into it like a total dupe.

He stopped at the cottage to grab his passport and stuff a few clothes into an overnight bag. Fifteen hours later, he was in Ibiza partying his way through a stream of worldly and cynical European girls, vowing to never let another woman hook him the way Layla had. The pain didn't go away, but after two weeks it lessened to the point that he felt he could face Layla and Andrew without doing them physical harm.

His plan had been to move to New Haven earlier than he needed. Now that Layla had chosen Andrew, there was nothing keeping him in Pittsburgh. But when he stopped in to get his things, he found the house in an uproar because Layla had fallen down their main stairs, and had only come out of her resulting coma the night before his return. Afraid of a lawsuit, his father forbade Andrew to have any further contact with Layla, and to Nathan's surprise, his twin had tersely agreed.

Despite Nathan's anger at her, he had to tamp down the urge to visit her himself. He couldn't stand the thought of lovely and vibrant Layla stuck in a hospital bed, having sustained multiple injuries. He had almost convinced himself to go see her against his parents' wishes, when her father had come to the mansion and threatened them with his bogus assault charge.

As his father had written hers a check, Nathan also wrote Layla off, shuttering his heart against her, and leaving for New Haven just a couple of days later. He didn't see or hear of her again until she came storming back into his life three months ago, reigniting his obsession with her, simply by revealing she had completely forgotten her betrayal and had no idea how deeply she had hurt him.

But now he could feel her slipping through his fingers again, and this time it was no one's fault but his own. That morning at work, he couldn't concentrate on the business contracts he'd been sent for review. He snapped at Kate more than once. He even hung up on one of his vice presidents—all because Layla had him so twisted up inside.

He couldn't let her stay in Pittsburgh, but at the same time, he couldn't figure out how to let her go.

Kate interrupted his brooding by buzzing into his office. "Mr. Sinclair, your sister-in-law is on line one."

"Send her to voicemail."

"She says it's urgent," Kate answered.

He rolled his eyes. Knowing his sister-in-law, she was panicking about some detail of the ball. But he took it, just in case it had something to do with Andrew.

He pushed line one. "Diana, what do you want?"

Diana's voice came down the line, crisp but

distraught. "There's a black woman sitting in our receiving room. She says she's Andrew's ex-girlfriend, and that she'd like to talk to him. Do you know anything about this?"

Fury exploded in his chest. "Keep her there," he said, barely able to speak.

"Nathan, what's going on?"

"I'm coming right now. Keep her there, dammit."

He threw the phone back in its cradle and rushed out of his office without a word of explanation to Kate.

CHAPTER SEVENTEEN

LAYLA grew increasingly anxious the longer Andrew's society blond wife, Diana Sinclair, stayed gone. Maybe she shouldn't have introduced herself as an ex-girlfriend of Andrew's. But if she hadn't, she ran the risk of Diana finding out later, and it seemed disrespectful to not only show up at the woman's house out of the blue, but also to lie about who she was—especially if they were having marital problems like Jessica had said.

Diana responded to her introduction with a slightly nonplussed blink and she'd invited Layla in and even offered her a cup of tea.

"You have a lovely home," Layla said, following her into the receiving room, which was done up in tasteful French country decor, with a butter yellow and dark blue color scheme.

Layla though about Nathan's loft. The weekend before they'd gone shopping in the nearby Southside Works, and she'd convinced Nathan to buy some bright yellow accent pieces and a few electric blue end-tables to break up all the black and grey going on in his converted warehouse loft. The insertion of a few pops of color had transformed the apartment, and even Nathan admitted it made his home look a lot more welcoming and a lot less industrial. She had been hoping to convince him to paint the kitchen cabinets red before she left, but now she wasn't even sure Nathan and she would still be talking after the terrible weekend they'd had.

"Thank you," Diana said. "We inherited the house from Andrew's parents, but I've tried to make it our own over the years. I'll be right back with that tea."

Layla had been a little surprised she hadn't called a servant to bring it to them. The mansion had looked huge from the outside, like the kind of place that took an entire staff to run it. And something told her there should be servants lurking around somewhere. Perhaps it was instinct, or maybe it was even a memory trying to work its way to the surface.

Either way, Layla felt vaguely unsettled as she waited for Diana to return. Was Andrew here? Would she finally get the answers she'd been seeking? Did she even want to know, she wondered. The fact that Nathan had done so much to keep her from finding out what happened back then scared her.

At the opera fundraiser, she'd nearly had to restrain Jessica from going after Nathan herself. "He tricked you into dating him?" she'd said. "He used your lost memory to get you into his bed?!"

"No," Layla said, still trying to wrap her head around the fact that she had dated Andrew and not Nathan. "That's not exactly how it went down."

As furious as Layla was with Nathan, she knew a few things Jessica didn't. First of all, she didn't hate anybody. She might have deeply disliked Nathan back in the day, but she couldn't see herself openly hating on anyone. However, when they'd met, his hate for her had seemed real.

New scenarios began to play out in her head: Had Andrew been the man in her window seat dream/possible memory? Maybe Nathan hadn't approved of their relationship. Was that why he wanted her to leave town, to keep her away from his brother? Maybe his plan had been to get rid of her from the start, but he hadn't counted on their insane sexual chemistry.

In any case, one point shined bright and clear. She couldn't trust Nathan at all. If he could keep this much from her, for all she knew, he really was the person who had been threatening her about leaving town. She hadn't received any more threats since signing the contract with Nathan, so it made sense.

No, she thought. She couldn't let Jessica go out there and tell Nathan off. She couldn't even let him know she now knew what he'd hidden from her. What she needed to do now was find Andrew before her two weeks were up, and get the answers for herself. She'd somehow convinced Jessica not to say anything to Nathan.

"I need to talk to Andrew first, and then I'll have it out with Nathan. I don't suppose you know where Andrew lives or could get me his address?"

"Yes, same place he lived when you were dating him—at his parents' house. After his father died, his mother moved to Florida, and now Andrew and his wife live there. Nathan used to live there, too, when we were in college, in the guest house out back. But that was a long time ago, and I'm not remembering the exact address off the top of my head."

"Do you think you can find out? I'd really appreciate it," Layla said.

"Sure. It's probably just a matter of making a few phone calls."

They'd exchanged numbers and Layla, not wanting to tip Nathan off, had faked a migraine.

But Jessica hadn't called with the address until late Sunday night, which had forced the argument with Nathan.

It was too soon to confront him with what he had

done, since she still didn't know exactly what was going on, and knew he wouldn't tell her himself. But her emotions were warring inside of her. On one hand, she felt deeply betrayed. Apparently, she hadn't been good enough for his brother, but she'd do in pinch when it came to warming his bed for two months. On the other hand, she had gotten used to being with him every night. And even though she really, really didn't like him at that moment, her body still ached for him. She couldn't let him touch her again until she figured out his true intentions. But she also couldn't bear to be apart from him.

When he hadn't budged on her staying at her own apartment, it had almost been a relief to return to his bed, even if they were emotionally miles apart. She thanked the heavens when Jessica finally called with the address Sunday night.

On Monday, she took off from work and drove out to Fox Chapel, a swanky suburb of Pittsburgh proper, dotted by houses that sat on acres of land. She knew she couldn't just sit around and wait for Nathan to give her answers whenever he saw fit. But still, she felt somewhat guilty about going behind his back to find his brother. It didn't make any kind of sense to feel this guilt, but she did, and she couldn't shake the feeling that coming to this place where they'd both lived when she met them for the first time was a bad idea.

And as the time passed, fifteen minutes by her count, she became more and more rattled to the point that she got up and started walking around just to shake off the tension. That's when she saw it: the long, winding, white marble staircase, sitting just beyond an entrance opposite from the one she'd come in. She walked to the stairs, entranced by their cold beauty, and knew them immediately for what they were: the ones she'd fallen down.

They were housed within a much grander foyer than the one near the door. This one was so large, it could easily have doubled for a ballroom. In fact, it probably would be where they'd throw the Sinclair Ball in less than two weeks. Nathan mentioned it would take place at his family home, but back then she hadn't realized his brother lived there.

The stairs led to a landing, which she somehow knew led to a section of the house where Andrew and his parents had lived in large suites. Suddenly an image of her running across that landing flashed into her mind. Why? Was she running from someone? She couldn't remember. Only the sensation of falling through the air as she realized she'd miscalculated. She saw herself rolling down the stairs, her body hitting the unforgiving marble steps with sick, hard thuds until everything mercifully faded to black.

"Ms. Matthews?" a voice said behind her.

Startled out of her memory, Layla turned to see Diana standing in the entrance of the receiving room with a large cup of tea in her hands.

Layla frowned. It had taken Andrew's wife almost twenty minutes, just to make a cup of tea?

"Are you all right?" Diana asked, her brow furrowed.

Layla shook off the chilling memory of falling down the stairs and arranged her face into a pleasant smile. "Yes, I was just looking at your staircase. It's really, um...nice."

"Italian marble," Diana said. "Andrew's parents had it shipped in from Tuscany."

"Yes, about Andrew," Layla said. "Is he here? I

know it's not polite to show up unannounced like this, but I really need to talk to him."

Diana's lips thinned. "Are you having an affair with my husband?"

Layla's eyes widened. "No! Oh, gosh, no. I didn't even know he existed until I mistook Nathan for him."

Diana's eyes narrowed. "You said you used to date him."

"I did. I think. I mean this woman I met at a fundraiser told me we dated for almost a year." Now that Layla was explaining this out loud, she realized how crazy she must sound. "You see I had an accident, and I went into a coma, and I lost almost the entire year leading up to it. Nathan, Andrew—I don't remember them or anything that happened during the time I apparently dated Andrew. That's why I came back to Pittsburgh, to find out what happened that year. And that's the only reason I'm looking for Andrew right now. He's the only one who can give me the answers I need."

Diana set the tea mug down on a nearby end table. "Well, isn't this ironic, then, because I also have a few questions for Andrew, but unfortunately he's disappeared."

"Disappeared?" Layla said. "Since when?"

"Since the beginning of the summer. Supposedly he's called Nathan to check in, but I haven't seen him myself in almost three months."

Diana rubbed her wrist. It obviously agitated her to have to say this out loud.

"I'm sorry," Layla said.

Diana gave her a sharp look. "We were high school sweethearts, you know. When we met, he was a senior and I was freshman. Then he went to Carnegie

Mellon, and we continued to date. I was very in love with him, our families got along, and I was sure we'd get married. I even applied for early admission to Chatham, a local all-women's college, so I could stay near him. But then the night before my first day of college, he broke up with me. He said he didn't think it was right we had only ever dated each other and he wanted to explore other options."

She looked Layla up and down with frank disapproval. "I'd heard he started dating some freshman at his school soon after that. I'm guessing that was you. How long were you two together?"

Layla bit her lip. "I guess it was me, but I'm not sure how long we were together. Jessica thinks the entire school year. But I fell late that spring and there was some confusion after the accident. Then I moved to another state."

Diana's mouth twisted into a bitter smile. "He called me early that summer. I thought he had finally come to see reason, that we were meant to be together, but I guess, he called because you were no longer available."

Layla really didn't want that to be true. "I'm sure he loved you. And he probably still does," she said. "Maybe he's just going through a mid-life crisis. Maybe— "

The doorbell rang, and Diana turned to look toward it. "Excuse me," she said. "Our house staff is off on Mondays."

Layla waited in the receiving room, kicking herself. Not only had she gotten exactly zero of the answers she'd come for, but she'd also upset Andrew's wife. She could kill Nathan for having put her in this position.

But then as if conjured by her murderous thoughts of him, he came striding into receiving room, his face a thunder cloud of dark fury.

And Layla realized the woman she had just been feeling so sorry for had not only ratted her out to Nathan, but had also deliberately stalled her with tea to keep her there.

CHAPTER EIGHTEEN

NATHAN hadn't been sure what he would do when he got to the Sinclair mansion. Wringing Layla's neck came to mind, so did physically removing her from the state, so she would never be able to make him feel this way again. He was sick of waiting for the betrayal. He knew if his brother so much as saw Layla, who was and had always been the complete opposite of the woman he was now planning to divorce, he'd fall back in love with her. And once he found out Layla hadn't had anything to do with her father's blackmailing scheme, it would all be over. Layla, for her part, would only see Andrew as everything Nathan wasn't—nice, ethical, and almost as considerate as she was. They'd be the "perfect couple" again, leaving Nathan to fester in a pool of jealousy and rage.

No, she needed to leave Pittsburgh before Andrew returned to initiate his divorce. She'd leave that very night if it were up to him. But when he walked in to the receiving room and found her standing there, not even in her scrubs, which she must have changed out of as soon as she cleared the apartment, his mind went red.

He stalked over to her. "What are you doing here?" he asked, grabbing her by her upper arms.

She yanked one arm free and used it slap him, so hard the resounding crack of her hand hitting his face split the air. "No, you don't get to be mad," she said to him. "You deliberately misled to me. You used me, and the only reason you're angry is because I found out."

The rage morphed into something else then, something as ugly as the accusations she was throwing at him. He grabbed the wrist she'd used to slap him, and when she tried to yank it away from him, he threw her over his shoulder, not caring how it must have looked to Diana.

"Put me down." She banged her fists against his back as he carried her out of the house and back to the guest cottage, which Andrew and Diana still hadn't updated from the days when he lived there.

It looked exactly the same as it had back then, down to the framed 70s movie posters on the living room walls. He didn't put her down. He didn't even break his stride as he fireman carried her through the house. He didn't stop until he deposited her on the bed. Then he got on top of her before she could sit up, straddling her and pinning her wrists above her head with one hand.

"Say you belong to me," he said.

"Let me go," she said. "I can't believe you did that! Diana probably thinks we're both crazy right now!"

"I don't care," he growled. "Say it."

"No, I don't belong to you! I don't belong to anyone but myself." She struggled against his vice grip on her hands. "And maybe Andrew back in the day. But you forgot to mention that, didn't you?"

Rage went off like a bomb in his head. "You are mine," he said. "You were always mine."

He reached underneath her leggings and curved two fingers into her hole, which despite her anger was already warm and dripping. "You didn't get this wet for Andrew."

She looked away, obviously frustrated her body was responding to him even when she didn't want it to. "How would you know?" she asked him, through clenched teeth. "Maybe I did get wet like that for Andrew. Maybe I got even wetter. Maybe all of those sexy dreams I had were about him."

"Don't say that." He kissed her roughly, his fingers still working inside of her. "Don't ever fucking say anything like that to me ever again."

"I'll say whatever I want," Layla said. "I'm sick of being nice to you when all you do is lie to me. I can't wait to leave this city and you behind."

His soul screamed when she said that. "No, you belong to me. You're not like this with anyone else. Prove it, come for me right now."

Layla bit her lip and squeezed her eyes shut, obviously trying to fight of the coming orgasm. But it was too late. He could already feel herself clenching around his fingers. She moaned in embarrassed protest, but came anyway, underneath him, still dressed in all her clothes, with nothing but his hand inside of her.

Now he unfastened his own pants. "I shouldn't have let you go three days without this." He released his penis, which had been rock hard since he found her in his brother's receiving room. "Look at how bad you want me now. You're hot and begging for me."

"Fuck you," she whispered.

"No, I'm going to fuck you until you say what I want to hear." He pulled her tank top over her head, then used it to bind her wrists to one of the posts that made up the bed's headboard. "Then maybe I'll let you fuck me, but not until you admit you're mine. Not Andrew's. Mine."

***

When he said that, Layla could feel herself

growing slick with want for him again. She couldn't believe it. As much as she despised him right now, she still burned to have him inside of her. His fingers hadn't been enough. Nothing but having him fully embedded in her folds would be enough to satisfy her aching need.

But she shook her head against the rough desire burning through her, making her breasts feel heavy inside her bra, which he then proceeded to strip off of her. It was gone before Layla could even think to protest its removal. He took one pebbled nipple in his mouth, swirling his tongue around her large aureole, and applied so much pressure with his clamped lips that it walked a thin line between pleasure and pain.

She arched underneath him and he responded by pushing a knee between her thighs, making her open wide for him before he slipped inside of her with a long, slow thrust that set her teeth edge it felt so good. He lifted one of her legs over his shoulder, angling himself so he hit her G-spot every time he rocked into her. Then he stared at her hard and angry, until she came a second time.

"How many times do I have to make you come before you admit it?" he asked.

She stared back at him then, eyes defiant. "You might be able to control my body, but you don't control me. I had every right to come here and ask questions, especially if your brother and I used to date. I don't know why you want to keep us apart, and I don't care, but I'm not going to stop looking for him until I find out what happened ten years ago."

She had thought he was angry before, but nothing compared to the look that came over his face when she said that.

Without warning, he pulled out and flipped her

over. Her tank top stretched and twisted to accommodate her new position, and the next thing she knew, he'd pushed her butt into the air, entering her from behind, his passage ensured by the fact that she was dripping wet from the two times she'd already come for him.

"You want to know what happened?" he asked from behind her.

But when she tried to raise up to look back at him, he pressed her chest into the bed, pinning her there even as he stoked the fire inside of her with his merciless thrusts. "No, stay there."

She wanted to fight him on this, but he felt so thick inside of her, filling her up again and again as he slid in and out of her wet tunnel. She had to use all of her concentration to resist coming a third time.

"You want to know what happened?" he asked again, from his now fully dominant position over her.

"Yes, I want to know," she said, tearing up. He wasn't just punishing her for going behind his back to find his brother, he was humiliating her, and she was letting him, because Nathan, more than anyone she'd ever met, made her feel powerless, like she couldn't control her thoughts or body when he was in the room.

He bent over her, fingering one of her nipples as he stroked into her with slow, deep thrusts. "Here's what happened. You dated Andrew, and pretended you were too good of a girl to let him touch you. But one night when he was out of town, you claimed to love me, let me fuck you in that window seat you dreamt about, then we moved to this very bed, where I fucked you two more times. Then when Andrew returned the next morning, you went right back to him like nothing had ever happened between us. Because you are a beautiful liar, who used to get off on having two brothers chase after you before you fell and conveniently forgot every duplicitous thing you had ever said or done to me. That's what happened."

Even without having her own memories of the events, she knew what he said to be true as soon as the words came out of his mouth. And she understood now the vague feeling of guilt that always cropped up when she tried to get him to talk about their past.

She again tried to look up at him, but he kept her pinned, breasts pressed to the cool covers, while he rutted her from behind, like an animal. Finally he yelled out and spilled into her, nearly overflowing her hot tunnel with his load. She came, too, then, unable to fight it any longer, and she tremored around his cock, all but drinking in his seed as he released wave after wave of it inside of her.

She thought that would be the end of it, but he remained hard inside of her. "Say you're mine," he whispered, his voice harsh and ragged.

***

Nathan knew he should have let her go after the third time. He had never taken any woman that roughly, and he realized he was out of control at this point. If he had any sense of self-preservation, he'd get up, zip his pants, leave the room, and put as much distance between him and this woman as possible, considering she drove him crazy with both lust and anger.

But the animal that was in control of him now wouldn't let logic intercede. He wanted her. He wanted her on his terms, without fear of having his brother steal her away again. "Say you're mine."

"Nathan," she said, gasping for air underneath him. "Please let me up."

Coming back to himself a little bit, he released her, pulling out of her and sitting back. Then he waited to see if she would say the words he needed to hear or if he'd need to provide her with yet another example of how very much he owned her body.

But when she sat up and turned to face him, her wrists still bound to the bed post, he realized his mistake, because there were tears in her eyes. And just like that, she reversed the power between them.

"I hurt you," he said. He released her hands from the tank-top handcuffs. "I'm sorry I did that. I'm sorry I hurt you."

"No." She folded her arms over her breasts and clasped her hands underneath her chin. "You didn't hurt me."

"You're lying. I did hurt you."

But she guided him down to the bed, and arranged it so they were facing each other with their heads on separate pillows. "I just want to look at you. Just lay here with me, okay? You didn't hurt me, I promise you. I would have told you to stop if you were hurting me."

"Then why are you crying?" he asked. On one hand he wanted to bury himself inside her and punish her some more for seeking out his brother behind his back—again. On the other hand, he felt like punching himself for causing her any pain. It was hard, he was discovering, to feel like someone's victim and protector at the same time.

"I'm crying because I hurt you," she said. "And I'm

sorry."

She scooted closer, and pressed her soft lips to his. "I'm sorry," she said again.

And this time it was she who guided his him inside of her, stroking her hips against his in penance for something she couldn't remember doing. "But I know myself well enough to know I didn't lie to you. My father used to tell the women he dated that he loved them just to score more money off of them. He broke a lot of hearts, and I promised myself back when I was a little girl that I would never pretend to love someone. Love is a beautiful gift, and I don't toss that word around lightly. I never have. So if I told you I loved you, I must have meant it."

"Don't say that." He shook his head, fighting the ray of hope that lit up his heart before he could contain it.

But she shook her head, too. "No, I have to say this, because you need to understand. I love you now, and I'm sure I loved you then. I'm sorry if I wasn't strong enough to leave Andrew for you."

Compared to the angry, primal sex they'd just had, Layla's soft velvet strokes against his dick shouldn't have excited anything within him. But he felt his balls tightening as she conquered him with the one word he hadn't been prepared for.

"You don't have to love me back," she said, her breath hitching as her own orgasm built inside of her. "I understand why you can't love me the way I love you, but I need you to know how I feel. I do belong to you, but only because I love you now, and apparently, I loved you back then. I'll always love you, Nathan."

That declared, she kissed him, and his orgasm burst through him, touching every nerve in his body before he released into Layla, kissing her back with all the love he'd been trying to deny ever since she'd come back into his life.

CHAPTER NINETEEN

FOUR times proved to be too much for Layla, and sleep began to overtake her, even as Nathan pulled out of her. But he gently shook her awake before she could drift off and whispered, "Let's go" in her ear.

She pulled her clothes back on, feeling awkward and raw inside and out. She could barely look Nathan in the eye after what has just transpired between them and when she rose from the bed, her thighs and vagina protested, sore from not one but four sessions of the most intense sex she'd ever had.

She peeked sideways at Nathan in the car, but his face revealed nothing.

"I'll send Kate for your car," he said. Then he didn't speak again until they were back at his loft and she'd come out of the bathroom after taking a shower.

"You're in pain," he said, noting her ginger steps as she walked over to the bed.

She winced. "Yeah, we might have overdone it."

"I'll take a shower, too, then we need to talk," he said.

She was already curled up under the silky sheets, her head nuzzled into his glorious pillows. "Okay, I'll be right here when you get out," she said with a yawn.

After the terrible weekend of sneaking around and keeping things from Nathan, and the big confrontation in the Sinclair guest cottage, she must have truly been spent because she fell asleep at once, not waking up until several hours later.

This time when she opened her eyes, though, she was greeted with the surprise of a gray wall blocking her view of the rest of the loft. Nathan had shown her the retractable walls cleverly embedded into slots strategically situated in various spots around the place, so he could create rooms on the fly around the office space or the bedroom. But so far they'd never had occasion to use them. For someone who claimed to value his privacy, Nathan had yet to really insist on it.

But when she woke up, the wall had been pulled and she could hear Nathan talking to what sounded like two men on the other side of it. She climbed out of bed. Her nether regions still felt a little raw but her curiosity won out over any physical pain she was experiencing at the moment.

She slipped a sundress over her head and tied her hair back in a low puff before venturing out into the common area where Nathan sat in the living room with two silver-haired men dressed in suits. When they saw her, they both stood.

"Ms. Matthews," one of them said. "It's my pleasure to meet you. I'm Bernard Wright and this is my partner, Graham Hastings. We're Mr. Sinclair's lawyers."

"Hi," Layla said. "It's nice to meet you both." But she gave Nathan, who remained seated on the couch, a quizzical look. What were his lawyers doing at his apartment on a Monday night?

"We're done here," Nathan said to them. "You can go."

The two men nodded. "If you have any questions about the paperwork, just give us a call at the office," Graham said.

"Would you like to stay for dinner?" Layla asked. "It's the least we could do. You came all the way over here."

Nathan regarded her with amusement in his eyes.

"They can't stay, Layla. They were just about to leave."

"Yes," Bernard said. "It's best we go, but congratulations Ms. Matthews. Again, call us if you have any questions about the paperwork."

He indicated what looked like four copies of a rather thick contract sitting on the coffee table. Then, despite their invitation to come to them with questions, they headed out the door before Layla could ask them any.

"What was that all about?" she asked Nathan once they were gone.

"How are you feeling?" he asked. "Still sore?"

"Just a little bit," she said. "But why did your lawyers just congratulate me?"

"Sit down, Layla." He moved to the side, so she could take a seat beside him.

Layla sat but she stared at the contracts as she did so until it occurred to her: "Oh my gosh, are you letting me out of the other contract? Is that what this is all about?"

"Yes," he said. "This contract makes the other one null and void."

She gasped and threw her arms around his neck, kissing him all over his hard-edged face. "Thank you! I'm so happy you're doing this."

"Wait, Layla." He stopped her kisses, cupping her shoulders to keep her in place. "This contract makes the other one null and void on the condition that you marry me."

She leaned back from him. "What?"

"It's a very generous pre-nup. If you sign it, not only will the other contract be null and void as long as you're my wife, but in the event we end up divorcing, you'll be very well taken care of."

"Oh, wow, you're seriously pitching this to me." Layla moved away from him, realizing the full extent of his plan. "You think if you let me stay without some legal claim, I'll leave you for Andrew."

He didn't answer, but the tic in his jaw was all the answer she needed. "And does the contract also have a clause that if we get divorced, then I still have to leave town?"

"I wouldn't care to share a city with my ex-wife, especially if she—" he broke off, but Layla didn't need him to finish to understand. If she left him for Andrew, then yes, she'd once again be forced to leave Pittsburgh.

She shook her head, "You really don't trust me."

"It's not about trust, it's about continuing this relationship under terms I can deal with."

She stood up. "No, it's about trust. I love you and you don't trust me at all. Why would you want to be with someone you don't trust?"

"I don't want to be you," he yelled, also standing up. "Don't you get it? No, I don't trust you after what you did, and because of that, I don't want to be with you. But I'm obsessed with you. If I could figure out a way to not be, believe me I would have employed it six ways to Sunday already. Sign the pre-nup, Layla."

And just like that, they were back in front of her apartment building, with him demanding she consign their relationship to a legal document. "No," she said.

He pointed at her, his face turning vicious. "Don't say no. You know how ruthless I can be. And you know I will get my way with this."

"Not this time," she said, pointing right back at him. "I understand what's going on now, and I'm not going to let you do this to us."

"This is the only way there can be an us."

"No, it isn't. Not if you decide to just trust me. I love you, now you have to trust me if you want us to be together."

He shook his head. "If you really love me like you claim to—"

"I don't claim," she said. "I do. I love you so much. My heart belongs to you, not your brother, not any other man. To you."

His face by this point had turned red with anger. "Then sign the pre-nup and marry me, goddammit."

"No," she yelled back. "Not like this."

They stood there at an impasse, both breathing hard. She was angry at him for making this so difficult, but she could sense he was angry at her for the exact same reason. At her job Layla was known for her easy ways, for her ability to be flexible and work with just about anyone from the crankiest patients to the despondent ones who didn't believe they'd ever get better. But Nathan had a way of finding all of her no-go zones. She couldn't give in to him on this, but she knew he also wouldn't cave.

Finally she said, "I'm sorry I hurt you ten years ago, but you can't keep punishing me. You either have to trust me or let me go."

He kept his eyes on the unsigned contracts, obviously too furious to speak.

Tears pooled in Layla's eyes for the second time that day. "Then I guess we've got our answer."

She began to walk back to the bedroom, prepared to get her things and wait out the rest of the contract period in her apartment. She suddenly couldn't bear this, being in love with someone who couldn't forgive her. "I'm going back to my apartment."

But before she'd even taken two steps, he wrapped his arms around her from behind. "No," he said. "We still have eleven days. You promised, and I'm assuming I can still trust you to keep your promises."

She closed her eyes. "Nathan, you said it yourself. You don't want me here. Don't you think it would be better if we had a clean break? If I leave now, then we don't have to keep torturing each other like this."

He turned her around in his arms, rubbing the evidence of his desire against her, which immediately caused her to swell with need, even though she was still sore from that morning. "I'd rather you keep torturing me," he said, running his lips along her neckline. "If you're going to run out on me, then you're going to have to break your promise, because I'm not letting you go before the move date."

He ground his erection into the front of her. "You drive me crazy with this, Layla. How can I still want you this much after two months?" He made it sound more like a curse than a question, and his kisses became more urgent.

He untied the sundress's straps and pulled the front down to reveal her dark brown breasts. His mouth covered one large aureole, laving it with his tongue.

But then he stopped, drew up straight, and headed toward the kitchen.

"What's going on?" she asked, a small anger rising in her chest. She crossed her arms over her breasts. Why would he start something he didn't plan to finish?

"Take of your clothes and lay down on the couch," he said, now in the kitchen. "I'll be right back."

Layla peeled the rest of the way out of her dress and did as he said, beyond confused. He soon returned with a glass full of ice cut into half moons, which he set on a nearby coffee table. Still, she felt vulnerable and exposed lying there naked on the couch.

But her embarrassment faded, when he turned to her, his eyes filled with smoky lust as he took her in. She could feel how much he appreciated the sight of her, even before he ran his large hands down her body until he reached the hair-covered mound between her legs.

"You're so warm," he said, palming it gently. He ran his thumb over the bud of her clit, and she responded with a sharp intake of breath. "And already wet, even though you're still sore from this morning. Bad Layla."

She bit her lip, arching into his hand. She didn't care if her response made her bad…just that he continue sending delicious thrills through her like this.

He took her hand and placed it over his erection, which was straining against his pants. "Feel how hard it makes me to see you like this. Now we're both in trouble, because I need to be inside of you, and you're still sore from this morning."

"It's okay," she said, lifting her hips in the hope of getting one of the fingers he was rubbing against her clit and outer walls inside of her. "Please, Nathan. I need you."

"You need me to what? I like hearing dirty words come out of your pretty mouth."

She squirmed against his hand. "I need you to fuck me. Please."

He continued to rub her outside walls and thumb her clit, but maddeningly refused to slip anything inside of her. She couldn't take it anymore. She reached for him, determined to throw him to the ground and climb on top of him herself. But he forcefully pushed her back down on the couch.

"I don't want to hurt you."

"Nathan, it's fine, just fuck me, please."

Usually begging was enough to get him moving, but this time he ignored her. He even withdrew his hand from her and used it to fish a piece of ice out of the glass, which he popped into his mouth.

Now he was taking a break to suck on a piece of ice? She began to sit up, but before she could, his hands were on her shoulders again, pressing her back into the couch. He dipped down below her waistline, and the next thing she knew, something cold entered her sex and started lapping at it. After a moment, she realized it was Nathan's tongue. With the piece of ice in his mouth, he ran the ice between her throbbing folds, heating her and numbing her sore vagina at the same time, before sucking her clit in between his cold lips. She gasped with pleasure. She'd never felt anything like this before, and the deep cold kiss sent shivers of electricity through her entire body.

"Oh, yes, Nathan. That feels so good." She grasped his hair and opened even wider for him. "Please don't stop."

But he did stop, lifting up to inform her with a smirk, "The ice has melted. You're too hot down there. Maybe if I do this..."

He fished out another piece of ice, but instead of putting it in his mouth this time, he used his left hand to spread her labia's lips, and slipped the ice past her walls, into her blazing hot passageway.

Layla's heart nearly stopped, the sensation was so shocking. Then he started entering her as well, pushing the ice further and further into her, until both he and it were completely embedded inside of her.

It felt like her pussy was steaming. And her brain short-circuited with pleasure, unable to handle the opposite sensations of hot and cold. "Nathan! Nathan! Nathan!" she screamed.

He grunted and gritted his teeth, holding himself still above her. "You're so tight. I'm trying to go easy on you, but you're making it hard for me to stay in control here."

"No, Nathan, please move. I need you to move." She rocked her hips up against his, so there'd be no mistaking how much she wanted this.

Finally he started moving inside of her, and it wasn't long before she found herself on the edge of a climax that built up inside of her like a freight train. The orgasm hit her so hard she screamed, biting into Nathan's shoulder as he yelled and came himself.

He collapsed on top of her, and Layla's heart suddenly flooded with relief. Thank heavens he'd made her stay. Eleven days meant maybe they still had time. Maybe he'd come to see how much she loved him and let her out of the contract, so she could stay with him. Maybe he'd even love her back, despite what had happened between them in the past.

But then he said, "Layla, I need you to sign that contract."

And they were right back where they started.

"No," she whispered. "I can't."

"You can."

"Let's not talk about it anymore," she said. "Let's just enjoy the time we have left, okay?"

He grew quiet, but she could already tell he was plotting another tactic to get what he wanted. She just hoped she would be strong enough to withstand it.

CHAPTER TWENTY

THE MORNING of the Sinclair Ball, Nathan could be found in his office, staring out of his panoramic window, still trying to figure out how to get Layla to sign the pre-nup. So far, he'd cajoled her, threatened her—he'd even offered to double the amount of her pay out in case of a divorce. But she just kept denying him, insisting he let her stay in Pittsburgh, so their relationship could progress naturally. Like a natural progression was even possible given their history.

The problem with Layla was she truly believed everything between them could be solved with love and trust. However, before she'd lost her memory, she'd come to the conclusion Andrew was a much better choice for her. And even if she had been serious about loving Nathan, as she now insisted she must have been, she had obviously loved Andrew more.

And though he'd harbored a great bitterness against her all of these years, he couldn't say he didn't understand her logic. Andrew was the good guy, even-keel and intelligent. Why wouldn't she want to be with him as opposed to Nathan?

Nathan understood Layla couldn't stay with him and be faithful to him without a legal document like the one he'd put forward. He was insisting on the contract for her own good. If they weren't married, if and when she and Andrew met again, then she'd fall for him. She'd feel guilty about it, but she wouldn't be able to deny how well they fit together, how little they argued compared to her and Nathan, and eventually she'd choose Andrew.

But if she signed the contract, if she formally

promised to stay with Nathan, her out-of-whack honor code wouldn't allow her to switch brothers. He knew Layla, and he knew she'd ask for a divorce and leave town on her own before she ever violated her marriage vows. If she signed the contract, she might hurt him again, but it wouldn't be with Andrew.

However, Layla didn't get that. She wanted him to trust her, but she didn't understand she couldn't be trusted when it came to Andrew.

"Brooding again?"

He looked up to see Kate standing in the doorway. "Yes, I suppose I am."

"She still won't sign the contract, huh?"

Nathan ground his teeth. "No."

Another strange side effect of his relationship with Layla had been a warming of his working relationship with Kate. Over the weeks, he'd asked his assistant to do so many things in regards to Layla, eventually she'd come to know more about the inner workings of their strange affair than anyone else.

She came in and sat down in one of his guest chairs. "I've been thinking about that," she said. "How exactly did you ask her to marry you?"

"I didn't ask her to marry me," Nathan answered. "I explained to her what the pre-nup entailed and then she spent the next two weeks refusing to sign it."

Kate nodded. "That's what I thought. Do you think you might catch more flies with honey?"

Nathan shook his head. "I'm not catching your meaning."

"Well, Layla's a sweet girl. And though your contract terms are very generous, maybe what she needs is a romantic proposal. For example, if instead of saying, 'Hey, Layla, sign this pre-nup,' you presented her with a ring and actually said, 'Layla, I love you, will you marry me' then maybe she'd say yes to the rest of it as well."

Nathan sat forward, liking where Kate was going with this, but..."I can't tell her I love her until she agrees to marry me."

She pursed her lips. "You're not in high school, Mr. Sinclair. There's nothing wrong with telling her how you feel."

"There's also nothing wrong with playing my cards close to the chest until I'm sure I'm in control of the game."

His secretary actually rolled her eyes at him. Two months ago, she wouldn't have dared. "Fine, then. How about just 'Layla, will you marry me?' Women really do like to hear the words."

Nathan nodded, warming up to the idea. "I could do it at the Sinclair Ball. Make it romantic."

"Exactly." Kate pulled out her smartphone. "Would you like me to pick out a ring for the proposal and let your sister-in-law know it will be taking place so we can schedule it into the program?"

"Sure, let Diana know, but you don't have to pick out the ring. Find a jeweler, and I'll go and pick it out myself."

Kate hesitated. "With all due respect, Mr. Sinclair, I know her taste. I think it's best if I pick out the ring."

Nathan smiled.

"What?"

"She's gotten to you, too. Three months ago you called security on her, and now you're insisting on picking out the ring and coordinating the proposal to make sure it meets Layla's romantic standards."

Kate rather uncharacteristically blushed. "Well,

part of my job is to make you look as good as possible. And like I said, she's a very sweet girl. I really don't think you could ask for a better wife. Especially if she has the right ring on her finger."

He smiled again. "Fine, you can come along. How about that?"

Less than thirty minutes later he stood inside Henne Jewelers, an upscale jewelry store in Shadyside, listening to Kate give the dapper man behind the counter instructions for the kind of ring they wanted. "Understated with a little flash. Maybe something that looks vintage but has some great detail like an emerald or a yellow diamond or maybe even a sapphire. But we'll need it within the next few hours, so it will have to already be in her size."

Kate's phone rang, interrupting her detailed list. She checked the caller ID. "Sorry, I have to take this. It's the movers I contracted for Layla's apartment."

She took the call and said, "This is Kate. Please hold" and hit the mute button, before turning to Nathan. "By the way, should I have them just move her things into a storage locker until we get her answer?"

"Good idea," Nathan said.

The jeweler started to set out a few engagement rings that matched Kate's requirements while Kate walked away to take the call. As Nathan surveyed the rings, he tried to imagine how each one would look on Layla's finger. Would it complement or overpower her scrubs and her soft casual weekend looks? He picked up a sapphire with a square setting and thought about the children they might have if they managed to stay together.

He smiled to himself thinking of a little girl with Layla's smile, or a boy with her bright eyes. The thought of being connected to Layla through their children warmed his heart and made him start thinking of that night's proposal not just as a means to get her to sign the pre-nup, but also as a possible step toward their future happiness. He had never thought of himself as the marrying kind, or the fatherly kind, or even the happily ever after kind, but looking at these rings, he saw it clearly. If Layla accepted his proposal, they would be happy together. Andrew or no Andrew. It almost made him wonder if he shouldn't let her out of the contract. If she married him, then maybe he'd be able to come to trust her without it.

Kate's return interrupted his thoughts. He immediately noted her face was pale and she held her phone in a white-knuckled death grip.

"Are you okay?" he asked.

"Could you give us a moment alone?" she asked the jeweler.

"Of course." The jeweler faded back into the woodwork, leaving them to their private conversation.

"What's wrong?" Nathan asked.

"The movers just opened up Layla's apartment and they found something disturbing."

Nathan stood up straighter, anger already working its way into his gut. "It was another threat wasn't it?"

Kate nodded. "This time spray painted across her living room wall."

"What did it say?"

Kate grimaced as if it physically pained her to have to repeat the words out loud. "Leave Pittsburgh, or I'll kill you."

***

That was exactly what it said as Nathan found out for himself fifteen minutes later. He stood in front of the large, spray painted message with the movers and Spencer Greeley, the private investigator he'd hired back in August looking on.

"I checked the security camera we had installed in the lobby, but the guy was good. Wore a hoodie and kept his face down," Greeley told him. "Other than that, the case has gone pretty cold. I'm doing extensive background checks on everyone who signed in at Ms. Matthews physical therapy center the day of the first incident, but so far no hits. No one who ever came into contact with Layla in a non-patient way and no one who'd wish her any harm. I'm almost done."

Fear for Layla's well-being fueled the hot anger in Nathan's gut. "Almost isn't good enough," he said. "I want full reports on everybody who came into the center by tomorrow morning. This maniac broke into her apartment. What if she had been here?"

Not waiting for an answer, he started walking back out to his car, his need to see that Layla was safe with his own eyes sudden and great. "I understand you're upset, Mr. Sinclair," Greeley said, running to catch up with him outside the building. "I'm doing the best I can, but there just aren't many leads here."

"I don't need your empathy," Nathan said. "I need you to do your job."

He turned to step into his car. He was about to call Layla when a call from Diana came through.

He picked it up, even though talking to his soon-to-be-former sister-in-law was the last thing he wanted to do right now. "What?"

Diana could barely speak, she was crying so hard. "Andrew's back in town," she said.

Nathan gripped the steering wheel. "What? Are you sure?"

"Yes, I'm sure, because the bastard just served me with divorce papers himself," she wailed. "And he said he knew Layla was back."

CHAPTER TWENTY-ONE

LAYLA spent the morning before the Sinclair Ball primping at an exclusive spa, which was followed by an afternoon hair and make-up appointment with Mark and Jacob. The good news was it took way less time to get her presentable than it had for the opera fundraiser. The bad news was she still hadn't decided what to wear to the event. She'd assured Kate over and over again that she was perfectly capable of picking out her own dress...then she'd left actually shopping for it until the last minute—the very, very last minute.

She hit a department store after her hair and make-up appointment and ended up putting two dresses, an elegant purple sheath and glittery black dress, on the card Kate had given her a few weeks ago to shop with. And by the time she pulled up to Nathan's building, she had less than an hour to spare before the car would arrive to take her to the Sinclair Ball.

She felt her phone, which she'd set to silent before her hair and makeup appointment, go off just as she was climbing out of her car with the two gowns. But, she didn't manage to dig it out from the bottom of her large purse before it went to voicemail, and when she checked the display window, she saw she'd missed five calls from Nathan.

She frowned at the number of missed calls and was just about to call him back when she spotted him standing outside his building. He'd gotten a hair cut, she noticed. It made him look even more suave in the tuxedo he was wearing, but she missed his bad boy CEO look.

"Did you forget your keys?" she asked as she

approached him. "That's not like you."

He didn't answer, just stared at her, which Layla supposed meant he wasn't up for being teased about forgetting his keys. He'd been a little on edge lately, due to the ongoing negotiations with the president of Matsuda Steel, who had been in town for three days now. Matsuda had promised Nathan he'd have a decision for him by tonight's ball. No wonder he'd forgotten his keys. This was his first international deal, he'd been forced to step in for his brother, and it all came down to tonight. Layla decided to cut him a little slack.

"I'm really sorry I missed all of your calls. I didn't know you were locked out. Here..." She handed him the two dresses and unlocked the fire door for them.

She noticed him hesitate, before saying, "That's okay."

"I thought we were supposed to meet at the Sinclair Ball," she said as they walked inside.

"We were?" he asked.

"That's what Kate said, but maybe I misunderstood." She tried to take the dresses from him, but he had his hand wrapped around the dress bags loop in a white-knuckled death grip. When she touched him, she could almost feel his agitation. "Look, I know you have a lot riding on this Japan deal, but it's going to be okay."

"Really? You believe that?"

She took his hand in both of hers. "Yeah, I mean, I know your brother bailed on you and maybe you didn't think you have the chops to negotiate a deal this huge. But you did it, and I know Matsuda's going to come back with the right decision."

He was silent for a long time before he relaxed his

grip on the dress bags' handles and said, "Thank you, Layla. You've always been very encouraging."

She took the dresses from him and laid them out on the couch in the living room area. "I'm not just being encouraging. I really believe in you. You've worked so hard on this deal. Matsuda would be crazy not to want you as a business partner."

He just stared at her, like she'd lost her mind, and she had the feeling somehow she was agitating him even further.

"You know what," she said. "Let's not talk about the Japan deal."

She peeled her tank top off over her head, careful to avoid messing up her freshly done hair or makeup. Then she took off her jeans as well. "Actually, I need you to help me pick out which dress to wear to the ball tonight."

He eyed her up and down, his eyes positively wolfish with lust. "Oh, I can definitely help with that."

She laughed and unhooked her bra, then laughed again when he drew in a sharp breath. What was with him? He was acting like he'd never seen her or her breasts before. Maybe, she thought with a fleeting sadness, it was because he knew this would be the last night they'd have together.

As the sadness of her impending departure washed over her, she wondered, not for the first time, if she should just give in and sign his stupid pre-nup. She honestly couldn't imagine spending the rest of her life with anyone else, and if her signing a document meant they could be together, maybe she should just do it, even if his distrust of her didn't exactly bode well for a healthy and lasting relationship—

Her thoughts were interrupted when Nathan

crossed the space between them, gathered her into his arms, and crushed her mouth to his.

***

"Hello, this is Layla. Please leave a message, and I'll call you back as soon as possible."

Nathan listened to Layla's message, which she of course delivered in a sincerely apologetic tone, for the sixth time in less than sixty minutes. "Layla, this is Nathan. Call me back as soon as you get this."

She still wasn't answering her phone, and his earlier fear was beginning to morph into true dread, so he checked in with Kate again.

Kate's search hadn't gone any better. "I called Jacob, and he said she'd already left. But he also said something about her still needing to pick out an evening gown. So I called just about every department store in the city, but that didn't turn up anything. So I called Spencer Greeley to see if he could trace the credit card I gave her to buy the dress. I knew I should have just picked one out for her," she fretted. "But she said she wanted to choose her own dress this time. Mr. Greeley said he'd see what he could do, but he was already working on another project for you due in the morning."

"I'm near my loft. I'm going to check to see if maybe she's there and just not answering her phone for some reason," Nathan said. "I'll call you back if she isn't, and you can tell Greeley to make the credit card his first priority."

A few minutes after hanging up with Kate, he was relieved when he pulled up to his building and saw the red Mini he'd bought Layla parked curbside. There was a small lot around back, but Layla claimed to prefer street parking in front because it was less fuss. When it came to everything outside of him, Layla always chose the less fuss option.

He took a leaf from her book, though, and parked his Maserati behind her car. His heart eased off the adrenaline as he entered the building and got into the elevator. But he couldn't quite allow himself to feel relief, not until he saw her with his own eyes.

However, when he opened the elevator doors, he did see her with his own eyes. And she was standing naked accept for a pair of panties, kissing his brother.

***

The kiss with Nathan was very nice, a little too nice. Alarm bells flared in the back of Layla's head. The kiss seemed familiar, like she'd experienced it before, but at the same time, it didn't feel quite right.

He smelled differently. Like simple soap and water as opposed to his usual expensive cologne. And though the kiss had started out with great passion, his lips were now gentle above hers, as if he'd be happy to just stand there kissing her for hours on end. And though she could feel his hard-on, none of Nathan's usual driving need seemed to be present. She couldn't remember him ever just kissing her like this, without touching her breasts or complaining about how crazy she drove him while seeking entry into her womanhood.

A nauseous feeling rose in her stomach. This man was a very good kisser, she realized. But he was not

Nathan.

She put her hands on his chest and pulled back from him, effectively breaking off the kiss. For a moment their eyes locked, hers confused, his glittering with some unnamed emotion. And then it hit her. She had finally found the man she'd been searching for since June. But she hadn't even recognized him as Andrew Sinclair until this very moment.

That's when she felt another presence in the space. They both looked up to find Nathan standing in the open doorway, his face a work of stone-cold anger.

"Nathan," she said. And the most eerie feeling of déjà vu overtook her.

She started to explain, but Nathan crossed the room in a lightning flash. And before she could stop him, he pulled Andrew away from her and punched him dead in the face.

CHAPTER TWENTY-TWO

"NATHAN, NO!" he heard Layla yell behind him.

Ten years ago, he had turned tail and run when he encountered a less-naked version of this exact scene, but this time he grabbed Andrew and punched him. He had been afraid of Andrew swooping in to steal Layla away from him before, but now he only knew determination. Layla was his woman, and he'd be damned if he let his brother steal her back twice.

He swung at Andrew again. The second punch also hit its mark, and it sent his brother toppling to the floor.

"Stop it," Layla said again. Out of the corner of one eye, he could see her putting back on her tank top.

Nathan ignored her, keeping his fists at the ready, while he waited for Andrew to get back on his feet, so he could hit him again. But Layla grabbed one of his punching arms, pulling it down with both of her hands and all of her might.

"Stop it," she said. "It's not what you think. I thought I was kissing you."

"What?" Nathan asked. The thought of his brother pretending to be him in order to kiss Layla sent another storm of rage through his entire system. "So you didn't—"

Andrew chose that moment to jump to his feet and blindside Nathan with a punch of his own. Nathan felt his lip split as his head whipped to the side with the impact of his brother's fist. He brought a hand up to his bloody lip and decided this time he was going to beat his brother within an inch of his life.

But before he could make a move on Andrew,

Layla was in front of him, pushing his brother away from him and saying, "Don't you dare hit him again. You stop this right now."

"He started it," Andrew yelled.

"Yes, because you tricked me into kissing you, which you had no right to do," she said. "Now back off."

"I had no right?" Andrew questioned. "Jessica told me he tricked you into dating him!"

"Who?" Nathan said, his killing rage giving way to confusion.

"One of your many ex-girlfriends. Remember? Apparently she ran into Layla at that opera fundraiser you attended."

Nathan cursed, remembering the pretty co-ed Layla had sent packing on their first and last double date. Why had he invited Layla to that ball? He should have kept her hidden away in his loft. It would have saved him a month's worth of drama if he'd just gone to the damn fundraiser alone.

Andrew continued. "Jessica emailed me a couple of weeks ago to tell me what you were up to. She said Layla was trying to find me. I would have come back sooner, but it took a while to get WiFi set up at the ranch, so I didn't get her message until a few nights ago. So I came back for the ball, served Diana with divorce papers, and now I'm here to find out why you tricked my ex-girlfriend, the only girl I truly ever loved, into sleeping and apparently cohabitating with you."

Nathan looked to Layla, who was now rubbing her temple as if this whole situation was giving her a headache. "You're in contact with Jessica?" he asked. "And you told her everything."

"No, not everything," Layla said. "But enough that I can see why she would have contacted Andrew. That

165

was very sweet of her."

"If by sweet, you mean meddlesome."

Layla glared at him. "By sweet, I mean she did what you were unwilling to do—help me get answers."

"Well, make sure to send her a thank you note after you leave town," he said. He knew he was being mean, but this was the exact scenario he'd been trying to avoid when he manipulated her into signing the contract. Now Jessica had ruined everything. Andrew knew about Layla, had served his wife with divorce papers, and was probably already plotting how to get his ex-girlfriend back.

As if reading his mind, Andrew's eyes gentled on Layla. "Jessica also told me you'd lost a year worth of memories after the accident. She said you were trying to find out what happened during that time. I wasn't sure how to approach you, and that's why I didn't tell you who I was right off the bat. I didn't want to upset you or scare you." His face turned red and he looked away. "I was trying to figure out how to tell you I wasn't Nathan, when you took your shirt off, and I got...distracted."

He stepped closer to her and rubbed her arms in a soothing manner. "I'm sorry for kissing you without your permission. But I can help you. And unlike Nathan, I actually want to help you remember."

It was a great speech, illustrating perfectly why Andrew had a reputation for being such a good guy. And it made Nathan want to punch him again, knock out teeth this time. "Take your hands off of her," he said, his voice low and menacing.

Andrew ignored him. "I was about to leave for the party. Come with me. We can talk, and I'll answer any questions you have."

"Won't your wife have a problem with that?" Nathan asked.

Andrew glared at him over Layla's shoulder. "My soon-to-be ex-wife you mean, and obviously she won't be attending the ball this year."

"Then who's going to handle hosting duties?"

"The party planner," he answered. "And, of course, I'll do my part to fill in any gaps left by Diana's absence."

"About time you finally decided to start doing your part. And what's this about a ranch. Is that where you were hiding?"

Andrew let go of Layla and turned to confront Nathan. "I've always done my part for Sinclair Industries. I'm the one who found us that deal and got Matsuda to the table. I had a few personal issues this summer, so yes, I stayed at a ranch in Montana for a while. And it was great, the best thing I've ever done for myself, which is why I ended up buying it. But at least I didn't spend the summer deceiving your ex-girlfriend, just so she'd sleep with me."

Andrew shook his head, his face filled with disgust. "You know, you've always had a bad reputation when it comes to women, but this is low, even for you."

"Yes, you're right," Nathan shot back. "I'm not a paragon of virtue like you, who hid out on a ranch all summer, then served his wife with divorce papers after which he immediately came looking for his ex-girlfriend."

"Diana and I were over long before I officially asked for a divorce. We never should have gotten married in the first place. I never would have taken her back, if she hadn't been there for me when…"

He caught himself and trailed off, but Nathan

finished the sentence for him. "If she hadn't been there for you after you abandoned Layla, then you never would have married Diana. That's what you're saying."

"I didn't abandon Layla," Andrew answered. "I honestly thought she was trying to sue our family. If I had known her father had been acting on his own, I never would have left her side."

But Nathan just shook his head. "You're a weak coward, and you don't deserve her."

Andrew's face turned red with fury. "And you think you do? The only reason she's with you is because she doesn't remember me. I'm the one she dated for a year. I'm the one who fell in love with her first ten years ago. You're just a parasite, preying on her head injury. Now if you'll excuse me, I'd rather help Layla get the answers she came to Pittsburgh for than stand here arguing with my good-for-nothing brother."

He turned back to the spot where he'd left Layla standing, but to both their surprise, she was no longer there.

"Layla," they said together.

"I'm over here," she said from behind the retractable wall that hid the bedroom.

Nathan and Andrew had been so consumed with their argument, they hadn't even noticed her pull the wall out, much less disappear behind it. But she now emerged from the hidden bedroom, dressed in a diaphanous purple sheath dress. She put Nathan in mind of a goddess as she walked toward them.

However, this goddess was positively radiating with anger. "I picked the purple one on my own while you two were fighting over me like two dogs with a bone."

Nathan folded his arms. Considering their history,

he saw no reason to pretend he was sorry for his behavior.

But of course, Andrew had to rush in with an apology, once again painting himself as the more upstanding brother. "I'm sorry. I came here to give you answers, and instead I ended up fighting with my brother. I guess not much hasn't changed since you saw us both last."

"Oh, it's changed," Nathan said. "Layla is mine now, and you don't have any business with her."

Andrew stiffened. "I don't want to upset Layla any further, so I'm going to ignore you." He turned his gaze back to her. "Does this mean you're driving to the ball with me?"

"No," Nathan said.

"Yes," Layla answered at the same time.

Nathan turned to regard Layla for the first time since he caught her kissing Andrew. "No," he said again, the command in his voice unmistakable.

"Yes," she repeated, her eyes steeled with resolution. "You don't own me, Nathan."

His entire body went stiff. It felt like she'd thrown a bucket of ice water at him. "And you asked why I don't trust you?"

He could see the steel in her eyes falter as guilt overrode her need for answers. "I'll see you at the ball," she said. "I promise."

"You also promised you'd attend the ball with me. If you go with Andrew then you're breaking that promise."

Again a falter. She looked from him to Andrew and back to him. And for a moment, he thought she'd give in, but then she drew herself up straight. "I guess I am breaking my promise then."

She turned to Andrew and said, "Lets go." Then she walked toward the still open door without a backwards glance.

Andrew followed her, but as he closed the door behind them, he met Nathan's eyes. And smirked.

CHAPTER TWENTY-THREE

"I STILL can't believe Nathan did this," Andrew said, his hands tight on the steering wheel of his Mercedes S-class, as they coasted through town on their way to Fox Chapel. "He's always been an irredeemable asshole, but this goes beyond his usual behavior. I could seriously maim him."

Layla peered at him sideways from the passenger seat. He'd been ranting about Nathan for the last ten minutes. "Are you done being angry with your brother yet?"

He threw her an apologetic look and covered her hand with his. The gesture was so automatic and familiar, she could easily imagine them driving in this exact same manner as younger versions of themselves. "I'm sorry. This is not the way I wanted our reunion to go. Nathan ruined that, too," he said.

Layla opened her mouth to answer, but he ended up correcting himself. "I'm doing it again." He squeezed her hand. "Okay, no more talk about that evil piece of shit I call a brother. Let's start answering your questions. I'm ready and willing. Ask me anything?"

"Really? Anything?" she said.

"Yes, really. You have to understand, Layla, I'm not usually like this. The Andrew you used to date was laidback and easygoing. I still am, but Nathan gets under my skin and brings out the worse parts of me."

She half-smiled. "Yeah, he has a way of doing that."

"But like I said, 'Enough about him.' Where do you want to start? With the fall?"

Layla nodded. "Yes, we could start there. Can you

tell me what happened that night?"

"Well, I don't actually know much. You'd come to visit me, but I was out to dinner with my parents. Apparently you asked one of the maids if it was okay to slip a note under my bedroom door. According to her you insisted on doing it yourself, and she liked you—" he broke off with a wry smile. "Everybody liked you. I'm sure the same is still true."

She demurred. "Not everybody," she insisted, thinking of whoever had spray painted her locker at work and the front door of her apartment.

"And still humble, too, I see." He gave her a teasing glance before continuing on. "In any case, she let you go up. Five minutes later she heard you scream, then she found you at the bottom of the staircase. From what the police could determine, you were distracted, missed the first step, and couldn't correct yourself once you started falling."

"So I wasn't pushed," Layla said.

"No, Nathan was in Ibiza, and it was night time, so there weren't any servants upstairs. But we paid your father off, because we knew how hard it would be to prove if you actually decided to take us to court. Also, at Sinclair Industries, we pride ourselves on our good community standing. My father didn't want a scandal."

Layla squeezed his hand. "Thank you for telling me. I really needed to hear what happened. And I'm sorry for any distress my father caused your family."

"No, I'm sorry for not coming to the hospital. If I'd known you were suffering from amnesia, it wouldn't have mattered that..." he trailed off with a shake of his head. "Believe me, I wouldn't have stayed away."

Layla gave his hand another squeeze. "I believe you. I think when you're not dealing with Nathan, you're a very upstanding and kind man. I can tell that."

Andrew let out a pent up breath. "I didn't realize how much I needed to hear you say that until you just did. I know Nathan made it seem like I was an uncaring pig for serving Diana and then seeking you out, but believe me, I struggled with the decision to ask Diana for a divorce. I keep my promises, and I made a vow to her, but we're just not good together. I like the outdoors, she prefers spa vacations. I want at least three children, she wants one, because she says she doesn't want to ruin her body. Hailing from two wealthy Pittsburgh families, it looked like we had enough things in common on paper to get along, but when it came down to who we really were as people, we were exact opposites. We would have made ourselves miserable keeping our promises if I hadn't ended it."

Layla thought of the look of disappointment on Nathan's face after she informed him she would be attending the ball with Andrew. "Yes, I understand we can't always keep our promises, even when we want to. I'm sure it must have been hard for you to take that step."

"It was," Andrew said. He stared ahead at the road. "But at the same time, it felt inevitable. You know why we went on our first date? Because our mothers were tennis partners and basically commanded us to go to the homecoming dance together. The entire time we've been together has felt like playacting to me. Of course we should date, we're perfectly matched. Of course we should get married, that's what our families expected from us. It's like I've been living this other man's life this entire time, except for when I dated you. I chose you. What we had was real, unlike the puppet show Diana and I were putting on."

Layla clamped her lips, her heart going out to both Andrew and Diana. "What a difficult situation," she said, rubbing his forearm with her other hand, much in the same way he had soothed her earlier.

She could see why Jessica had thought she and Andrew were such a great couple. Even though she didn't remember him, she could already feel the camaraderie they must have shared back in the day. Away from his brother, he was easy to talk to, and she could tell he shared many of her basic morals, unlike Nathan, who had to put effort into even being polite.

"Yes, I can tell you're a genuinely thoughtful and caring human being who takes his promises seriously," she said. "But I'm just confused about one thing."

"What?" he said. "Ask me anything. I'll answer it."

"Why didn't you tell your brother the truth after I fell?"

Andrew glanced over at her, confused. "What do you mean?"

"You see, he says I told him I loved him, had sex with him, and then went right back to you, but I don't think that's the way it went down. So I'd like to hear the real story now."

Silence and Andrew took his hand back, his formerly warm demeanor going as cold as a winter's day. But Layla refused to let him retreat behind the hard Sinclair wall.

"You're a good man, Andrew. I can see that clearly. And no matter what led you to keep the real story from Nathan, I'm sure you realize now that I deserve to know the truth."

More silence, but eventually Andrew said, "I didn't lie to him."

"I know you didn't," she said. "You're not the kind of person who lies. But maybe you let Nathan believe something that wasn't true and then I fell, and so you never bothered to set the record straight."

Andrew slammed his hand against the wheel. "It wasn't like that," he said. "After you spent the night with him, I caught you sneaking out through the house. You immediately burst into tears and said we needed to talk, so I took you up to my room, where you confessed everything. Then you said we needed to break up. I couldn't believe it, we'd been such a great couple, but you were just going to throw away everything we had after a one-night stand with Nathan. I pointed out to you that we hadn't even slept together. For all you knew, we already had what you thought you had with Nathan. So I kissed you, and you let me."

He shook his head at the memory. "Maybe you thought you owed me at least that much since you were dumping me for my twin brother, but when you didn't respond to my kiss, I broke it off. That's when we saw Nathan standing in the door. He walked away and you were about to go after him, but I held on to your arm and kept you there, trying to convince you that you were better off with me. By the time I let you go, it was too late, Nathan had already left for Ibiza."

His lips thinned. "The note you left under my door was actually one asking for forgiveness. You said you didn't want to come between Nathan and me and you felt so bad about the entire situation, you wouldn't be seeing either of us anymore. But I didn't find the note until after you fell, and a week later Nathan came back from Ibiza even more of an asshole than before he slept with my girlfriend. I figured he didn't deserve to know the truth. And then your father tried to blackmail us, and Diana showed up, and somewhere along the way I just lost my moral compass. I'm sorry."

He peeked sideways at Layla to see how she was taking all of this, but his contrite expression turned to one of surprise when he found her smiling from ear to ear, tears glistening in her eyes.

"You're happy?" he asked.

"Yes," she said. "Because now I finally know the truth. And the truth sounds exactly like me."

CHAPTER TWENTY-FOUR

"SO YOU'RE really planning to choose Nathan over me?" Andrew said as they pulled into the valet service line outside of his Fox Chapel mansion. Since it was technically his house, he could have parked in the separate garage structure. But Andrew, being the chivalrous type, had opted for the valet line since Layla was wearing heels.

Layla winced. "It sounds like I already chose Nathan a long time ago. It just took a while for me to get back to him."

"But he's not like you," Andrew said. "He's not a good person. Half the time, he's not even a decent person. You and I make sense, but you and he don't."

Layla turned to face him. "You know how you were describing your relationship with Diana as a puppet show? I think that's how I'd feel if I chose you. Logically we make sense, but no matter what, my heart belongs to Nathan."

Andrew gripped the wheel, his face the picture of bitterness. "Wow, leave it to Nathan to take the one girl I've ever really loved."

"He didn't take me," Layla said. "I chose him, too. We chose each other. And just let me point out, neither of you have been particularly honorable throughout this whole ordeal. You could have told him, but instead you let him spend years thinking I'd chosen you over him."

Andrew's jaw set just like Nathan's often did. For two people who claimed to be exact opposites, they had an awful lot in common, Layla thought.

"It's not like he really loved you back then or now.

He's probably just using you to get under my skin. He likes doing that, you know."

A certain serenity stole over Layla after Andrew accused Nathan of pretending to care about her just to get a rise out of his brother. Suddenly, she didn't just hope, she knew down to her very core this wasn't the case. "No, he loves me. He might not have said the words yet, but I know he loves me. I mean, he was so petrified you were going to steal me away, that he had a provision for it in the marriage contract he offered me."

"Wait a minute," Andrew said. "He asked you to marry him? Just to keep you away from me? And how is he not a bastard again?"

Layla reached across the space between them and cupped his face in her hand. "Don't be like this, Andrew."

"Like what," he asked, his jaw still clenched tight.

"Don't let my choosing Nathan make you bitter. There's a woman out there who truly is perfect for you, who will love you the way you deserve to be loved. Meanwhile, Nathan is your brother, the only one you have. Do you know how much I've always longed for a sibling? I won't come between you two, so you either need to give Nathan and me your blessing, or you need to tell me to leave town, so you two can get back to being brothers again. Whatever you decide, I'll do it."

The valet knocked on the window. Yes, it was Nathan's house, but they were holding up the valet line.

"Just a moment, please," Layla said through the closed window. Then she turned back to Andrew and waited for his answer.

***

Nathan changed into his tux and drove himself to the party after sending the car that came to pick up Layla away. But even with those delays, he arrived before she and Andrew did. Kate found him soon after he entered the ballroom, which was already crowded with the city's most powerful movers and shakers. The Sinclair Ball had been the exclusive event that marked that end of summer since before he was born. And making the guest list was considered an informal invitation to the local "It" list for up-and-coming business, political, and media stars alike.

"I've set everything up," Kate told him, covertly slipping the box with the emerald engagement ring they'd picked out inside into his tux pocket. "But where's Layla?"

"With my brother," Nathan answered between gritted teeth.

Kate's eyes went wide with surprise and sympathy. "So he's back?"

"Yes, and it doesn't look like there will be a proposal."

"Are you sure? Because Layla really did seem to sincerely like you…"

"I'm sure," Nathan said, his voice clipped. "I'm also sure I no longer want to talk about this particular subject. Thank you for setting everything up, now please undo it."

"Of course, Mr. Sinclair. Right away."

Kate rushed away to do his bidding. And he found himself wondering if he should have been a little more polite after all the work she'd done to make his proposal to Layla special. But then he caught himself, realizing he wouldn't even be thinking such a thing if Layla hadn't barged into his life and changed it so irrevocably.

He knew he should focus on the business of the party. Seek out Matsuda and see if it was yea or nay for the factory deal, but he couldn't get the picture of Andrew's smug smirk out of his mind.

Were they kissing now? Is that why they hadn't arrived yet? Maybe they had decided to skip the party altogether and finish their reunion in a hotel room. He could just hear Layla fretting over him seeing them together and suggesting she and Andrew not come so as to spare his feelings. It made him want to storm out of the party, track them down, and drag Layla back to his bed like a caveman.

But before he could act on that impulse, Kate reappeared at his side. "Would you like me to tell the movers to take Ms. Matthews things to Savannah after all?"

His first instinct was to say yes and congratulate himself for making her sign that contract before Andrew returned to town. But then he thought about the way Layla had glared at him when she defended Jessica's contacting Andrew. *"By sweet, I mean she did what you were unwilling to do—help me get answers."*

The fact was, Andrew had been right about him. Nathan had been angry at Layla for choosing Andrew ten years ago, but he'd also taken advantage of her memory loss, manipulated her into both signing that contract and staying in his bed, and now he was going to make it very difficult for her to be with his brother, a man who everyone would agree was probably much better suited to her, a man he'd stolen her from in the first place.

"No," he said out loud. "This stops now. Call Layla and tell her I'm cancelling the contract she signed. If she wants to stay in Pittsburgh, I won't stop her. Tell her..." The words caught in his throat, but it didn't make them any less true. "Tell her I just want her to be happy."

He could barely believe it, but it was true. For once, Nathan Sinclair cared about someone else's happiness more than his own.

***

Despite the valet's presence outside of the window, it still took Andrew a while to answer her ultimatum. But eventually he said, "Fine, if you're really that in love with him, I'm not going to get in your way. Go be with him."

Layla gasped and clapped her hands together. "Really?"

He rolled his eyes, looking both amused and aggrieved. "Yes, really Layla. Now get out of the car before I change my mind."

She didn't have to be told twice. She jumped out and dashed into the party. There was a long queue at the door, but Layla spotted Kate talking to the woman with a clipboard at the front of the line—probably the party planner Andrew had mentioned earlier. She ran over to them.

"Hi, Kate, I hate to skip the line, but I really need to find Nathan."

Kate's face lit up when Layla said this, and to Layla's surprise the older woman pulled her into a tight hug. "Oh, I knew you would pick Nathan. I never should have doubted you."

But then something else seemed to occur to Kate. She drew back with a worried look on her face. "Oh that means, I'll still need to…" She cut her eyes to Layla, but didn't finish that sentence. "Yes, go right on in, dear. I'll take care of everything else."

Layla wondered what the "everything else" was all about, but her urgent need to find Nathan and say yes to his marriage proposal overpowered her curiosity. After giving Kate's a quick arm squeeze in thanks, she ran inside. However, before she could make it from the receiving foyer to the main foyer where the ball was being held, a small hand grabbed her arm.

Layla turned around to see Diana. The blond was dressed appropriately in a tasteful black silk gown, but she wore no makeup and her long hair hung in a tangled mess.

"Oh, Diana, hi," Layla said. "I thought you weren't going to attend the ball this year."

"No, I wasn't, but I decided to rally," Diana said, her voice quivering. "Could you join me in the library? It's right over here."

Worried about Diana's obviously fragile state, Layla followed her into a large room right off the foyer, and closed the door behind them. She took a moment to note the window seat against the far wall. That must have been where she and Nathan first made love.

But then she turned her attention back to Diana, who had moved to a position behind a large heavy oak desk. There was something off about her eyes. She looked to be on the verge of tears but also on the edge of a scream.

Layla's heart went out to Andrew's obviously

distraught, soon-to-be ex-wife. "I know you're trying to rally, but it's probably not good for you to be here emotionally. Maybe you should let me take you to a hotel. If you give me a moment, I can borrow Nathan's car."

Diana opened a drawer. "I saw you and Andrew outside. You had your hand on his cheek. Are you getting back together then?" she asked.

"Oh, that," Layla said. "No, that wasn't anything. I was just saying good-bye."

"I don't believe you," Diana said, her voice suddenly going from quivering to hard as stone.

"It's true. There's nothing between Andrew and me. In fact, I'm in love with…"

She stopped when Diana pulled a gun out of the desk drawer and pointed it straight at her.

Fear sent her heart into her stomach with a metallic thud, and she took a step back. "Diana, what are you doing?"

Diana set her mouth in a grim line, before saying, "I told you to leave Pittsburgh. But you didn't listen to me, did you? So now, I'm going to have to kill you."

CHAPTER TWENTY-FIVE

NATHAN had been looking for Matsuda for the last twenty minutes, but so far between guests stopping him to thank him for hosting the ball and fellow businessmen stopping him to inquire after the Japan deal, he hadn't managed to actually connect with the man he hoped to be partnering with soon. So imagine his surprise when he found Matsuda at the edge of the party, talking in Japanese to his brother, who was now sporting a black eye, courtesy of the punch he'd delivered earlier.

Nathan rubbed his own jaw, which was beginning to swell from Andrew's own hit before interrupting their conversation without preamble, "What's going on here?"

"Ah, Mr. Sinclair," Matsuda said, switching to English. "I was just congratulating the other Mr. Sinclair. Our company has decided to accept your offer of partnership for a Japan site."

This was excellent news, what Nathan had been working toward all summer. But despite this, he turned to his brother and demanded, "Where's Layla?"

Andrew squinted. "I'd thought she would have found you by now. She jumped out of the car when we got here and went looking for you. She mentioned a contract."

"What?" Nathan said, even more confused now. But then it occurred to him: "Oh, she's trying to find me to thank me for letting her out of the contract. Kate must have already told her."

"What contract are we talking about?" Matsuda asked. "Is this Layla another business associate?"

"No," Nathan answered.

Andrew took him by the arm. "May we have a minute. There are some things I need to discuss with Nathan. Afterwards, we'll come back and toast our new partnership."

Matsuda bowed. "Of course."

Nathan barely had time to complete his bow before Andrew was tugging him away back toward the entrance foyer. "Okay, tell me about this contract," he said as soon as they were out of earshot.

Nathan told him about both contracts, figuring he deserved to know the truth about what had gone down that summer. "But I guess, I'm a better man than either you or Layla thought, because I'm done trying to control her with contracts. If you two want to be together again, I'm not going to get in your way."

Andrew shook his head with dawning realization. "You actually love her, don't you?"

"Obviously, I love her," Nathan answered. "And I want her to be happy, even if it's with you."

Andrew studied him, as if we were re-evaluating everything he thought he knew about his twin. In the end he heaved a sigh and said, "Okay, fine, I'll be your best man."

"What are you talking about?" Nathan asked.

"Layla was right about us needing to act like brothers again. We were actually doing okay before this summer, and we need to get back to that. So I'll be your best man at your wedding and somehow I'll forgive you for stealing Layla."

"I didn't steal her," Nathan said. "And what do you mean you'll be the best man at our wedding? What exactly happened between you and Layla?"

Andrew gave him a wry smile. "She chose you. I

stated my best case for why she should be with me, and she chose you anyway. Again."

Nathan went still. "What do you mean by 'again.'"

Andrew studied his tuxedo lapel, unwilling to meet Nathan's eyes. "I mean that kiss you saw ten years ago. It wasn't Layla and me kissing. It was me kissing Layla, trying to convince her not to dump me, in order to be with you."

Nathan's fists clenched. "You let me believe all this time that she'd chosen you?"

Andrew raised his hands. "Don't cause a scene," he warned. "I already have to explain to everyone why I have a black eye. And if you hit me again, my offer to be your best man comes off the table."

"You let me leave her in that hospital all alone, believing she didn't want me?" Nathan continued. "Do you have any idea how much I loved her, love her now?"

"Obviously I didn't, or I would have told you," Andrew answered. "And I can't believe you're trying to make me feel guilty for not helping you to steal my girlfriend."

"I didn't steal her. I loved her more than you did, and she loved me back. She chose me." Nathan said. Saying the words aloud filled him with a new wonder. He had spent all this time being bitter, but she had chosen him both then and now.

"Funny, that's kind of what she said."

Before Nathan could press him for further details, Kate came rushing toward them. "I saw Layla coming in, and I got everything reset up for the proposal." Kate frowned, looking over both shoulders. "But where is she?"

"That's what I'm trying to figure out," Nathan said.

"She must still be talking to Mrs. Sinclair—I mean Diana," Kate said, correcting herself with a glance toward Andrew. "I saw them go into the library together after Layla arrived. Diana looked upset and I think Layla was trying to comfort her."

They all exchanged knowing smiles. "Mystery solved," Nathan said. He cut his eyes toward his brother. "I'm going to have delay my proposal because my future wife is too busy comforting your future ex-wife."

Andrew shrugged. "Well, you know Layla. Maybe even better than I do at this point."

Nathan's phone vibrated in his tux pocket. After pulling it out, he checked the caller ID and saw it was Spencer Greeley. Maybe he had a break in the case.

"Excuse me," he said to Kate and Andrew. He walked away without waiting for their answer. At that point nothing was a bigger priority than keeping Layla safe. "Do you have something?" Nathan asked.

"I'm not sure," Sterling answered. "But I wanted to call you just in case. I finished going through the names on the sign-in sheet at Ms. Matthews' physical therapy center and one jumped out at me. Did you know your sister-in-law went into Layla's center a couple of times for physical therapy? Apparently, she'd sprained her wrist playing tennis."

Nathan's mind began putting two and two together, even before the detective had come to his conclusion. "Diana was there the day Layla was first threatened?"

"Yeah, she was. Might just be a coincidence, but I'm going to hack her credit card records to see if she's bought any cans of spray paint lately."

But something was already telling Nathan what

those records would reveal. Diana had lied. She had pretended to not even know who Layla was when she'd stopped by the mansion looking for Andrew. But Nathan was now certain Diana knew exactly who she was and had been threatening her accordingly ever since seeing her at the physical therapy center. He dropped the phone and started pushing through the crowd toward the library.

***

Inside the library, Layla tried to calm the screaming panic inside her mind and talk to Diana. "Diana, I know you think you saw something significant out there, but let me assure you, there is nothing between Andrew and me. I'm in love with Nathan."

"It doesn't matter who you're in love with," Diana said, coming around the desk. "He's in love with you. And if I can't have him, you can't."

"I don't want him. Seriously, I'm in love with Nathan."

Diana lips trembled into a bitter smile. "That's what you said ten years ago when you found me in Andrew's room."

Layla blinked, trying to process this new piece of information, even as a previously blocked memory unfolded in front of her mind's eye. "You were there," she whispered, remembering. "I came to deliver that note, and I found you in his room going through his things. I didn't know who you were, but I knew you didn't belong there."

"I was only trying to gather some information. I wanted to know who this girl was he'd been dating, and see if there was any way I could snatch him back from you." Diana said. "So I snuck in past the servants and I went into Andrew's room."

Layla shook her head. "Snatch him back from me? He broke up with you before he ever met me."

"I don't believe you," Diana said.

She had said the same words that night long ago, Layla now remembered, with that same crazed look in her eyes. Then she'd grabbed a Swiss Army knife off of Andrew's desk and came running toward her.

Layla's flight instinct had taken over at the sight of the knife bearing down on her and she'd run, only managing to get out one scream before she missed the step and went tumbling face forward down the stairs.

"It was you I was running from," she realized out loud.

"Yes, it was me, and I wish you had died. Then you wouldn't have come back to town to ruin my marriage," Diana said with venom in her voice. "Am I supposed to believe your return to Pittsburgh at the same time Andrew disappeared was just a coincidence?"

"Yes, that's exactly what you're supposed to believe," Layla said. "Because that's exactly what happened. I'm not in love with Andrew. In fact, when I came up to his room, I was just there to deliver an apology, because I had already broken up with him."

"I don't believe you! I don't believe you! I don't believe!" Diana screamed like a toddler throwing a temper tantrum. "All you do is lie. You pretend to be this innocent girl, but you stole Andrew from me twice." She cocked the gun.

And Layla began to feel real despair. This woman was going to kill her, for real this time, and before she had a chance to tell Nathan how she really felt and why she had chosen to go to the party with Andrew as opposed to him.

She had always had a thing about breaking promises and now she couldn't escape the irony. She had broken her promise, just once, and now she would be paying for that broken promise with her life.

Tears of frustration sprang to her eyes. "Okay, if you're going shoot me, no matter what, let me just say this. I love Nathan Sinclair. My heart belongs to him and it always will. If this ends badly for me, please let him know I said that."

Then Layla surprised her by running toward her and grabbing hold of the gun's barrel.

***

It felt to Nathan like the crowd grew thicker as he got closer to the library door, as if they were purposefully trying to keep him from Layla, his heart, his soul, the woman he wanted to spend the rest of his life with.

His father had always kept a revolver in a locked drawer in his desk. After inheriting the house, Andrew had not only kept the gun, but had also made a big deal of leaving it in the drawer, claiming that's what their father would have wanted.

Nathan knew Diana knew it was in there, and he felt sick with fear for Layla. He shoved people aside left and right, and cursed himself for never telling her how he truly felt, for never saying those three words during their two months together: I love you. He had been such a fool. He could only hope he wasn't too late.

Finally, he reached the library door and was just about to turn the knob, when a gunshot rang out on the other side of it.

EPILOGUE

FOR SOMEONE who hadn't thought she knew anyone when she first returned to Pittsburgh six months ago, it now seemed to Layla like she was most popular girl in town. Over 300 people had been invited to their wedding, and a few local media outlets, in the hopes that this would provide a natural close to the Diana Sinclair attempted murder/accidental suicide story, which continued to be an ongoing news cycle item four months later. Just about everyone had RSVP'd yes.

"It's a zoo down there," Carol said, returning to the master suite of the Sinclair mansion, where Mark and Jacob had set up the pre-wedding bridal base camp. Carol had insisted it was her duty as Layla's maid of honor to be nosy and go peak over the landing's banner to do an informal head count. "Did you invite the whole city?"

Layla laughed, which didn't please Mark, who was trying to apply the last of her makeup. "No, just everyone Sinclair Industries has ever done business with and the entire Matsuda board. I'm happy they all fit in the foyer for the ceremony."

A shadow passed over Layla's face. Many of their wedding guests had attended the Sinclair ball four months ago.

As if reading her thoughts, Carol said, "I wonder if they're here to celebrate your big day or to return to the scene of the crime?"

Layla decided to shrug it off. "I'm just happy they came."

Carol shook her head, "I can't believe you're still staying so positive after what happened to you."

Truth be told, Layla couldn't believe it either. She could still see Diana laying in a pool of blood, the light in her crazed eyes fading as she choked to death on her own blood. Sometimes she woke in the middle of the night, screaming for someone to call an ambulance just as she had the night Diana had accidentally shot herself while trying to wrestle the gun back from Layla. But it had been too late for Diana at the ball, and she'd met the same fate again and again in Layla's nightmares.

Luckily the last ten years had taught her to be grateful for anything she could actually remember. Even the bad stuff.

"A wedding seems like the perfect way to cleanse what happened here," Layla said. "Maybe it will bring everyone some measure of peace."

Carol came over to her hair and makeup chair and gave Layla's shoulder a comforting squeeze. "I just hope that fiancé of yours appreciates what a good woman he found in you."

"Trust me, he does," a voice said behind them.

They all turned to see Andrew standing in the doorway.

Layla smiled at him. "Mark, can you give me a second?"

"Sure," Mark said. "It's not like you have a big event we're trying to get you ready for or three-hundred guests waiting for you downstairs. We have all the time in the world."

Gently ignoring his sarcasm, Layla got out of her seat and walked over to Andrew. He gave her floor-length strapless wedding dress an appreciative once over. "You look beautiful, Layla."

"Thank you, but what are you doing up here? Shouldn't you be with Nathan?"

"I tried to explain to him you were perfectly all right and probably wouldn't get cold feet, but he sent me to make sure anyway." Andrew shook his head. "Said it was in my job description as the best man. But seriously, do you have cold feet? Because I'm ready and willing to take to you to Montana with me."

Layla chuckled. "No cold feet. They're very warm in fact. I can't wait to become Nathan's wife."

He snapped his fingers. "Well, damn. Never let it be said that I didn't try to give you an out."

Though his tone was joking, Layla knew this couldn't be easy for him. And she didn't think it was a coincidence Andrew had turned in his resignation only a couple of weeks before their wedding, announcing he'd decided to take up permanent residence at his ranch in Corral Springs, Montana and would no longer be living in Pittsburgh when they returned from their Fiji honeymoon. He'd even signed over the deed to the mansion to them.

Layla wrinkled her nose. "I still can't imagine you as a rancher. I mean, Nathan said you used to be really outdoorsy, but this seems like it's taking it a little far."

Andrew's eyes grew sad. "I can't stay here, not after what happened with Diana. And especially not after what she tried to do to you. It was all my fault."

Layla smoothed a hand over his cheek. "No it wasn't, Andrew. You were right to leave her. Diana was obviously unstable and at a deeper level you must have sensed that. You had no way of knowing she'd come after me. None of us even knew she knew me. She did a very good job of covering her tracks."

Andrew shook his head. "Still."

Layla gave him an understanding nod. "I know. We both have issues with guilt. Go to Montana. A few of my patients have taken long trips after they're done with physical therapy. I really hope it helps you to heal."

Andrew paused, looking like he was going to say something important, but instead opting for "Me too." He pasted a smile on his face. "Ready to get married to someone who isn't me?"

Layla remembered the way Nathan had gathered her into his arms when he found her crouched over Diana's body, screaming for an ambulance. "Don't look," he said, when she tried to turn back to see if there was anything else she could do.

"She's gone. Look at me, Layla," he'd said. "I love you. I've loved you from the first moment I saw you. No more contracts. I don't care about the pre-nup. I just want to spend the rest of my life showing you how much I love you."

And those words had brought her out of her hysteria. "I love you, too," she'd said.

A more formal proposal with the emerald ring had come a few weeks later during intermission at the first show of the opera's new season. But Layla would always think of her real proposal happening when Nathan snapped her out of her screaming fit by telling her he loved her, that he had never stopped loving her, that there would be no more contracts between them.

"I am definitely ready to get married," she told Andrew.

"Not before we finish your make-up, young lady," Mark said from his position at the makeup chair. "Now get back over here."

***

Four hours later, a limo dropped Nathan and Layla at The Renaissance, a swanky hotel in Downtown Pittsburgh. "Congratulations, Mrs. Sinclair," the driver said, handing her out of the vehicle.

Layla barely got a chance to say thank you, before Nathan took her hand from the driver and swept her into the hotel.

"You didn't say thank you," Layla said, rushing to keep up with him as he strode across the lobby toward the elevator banks.

"I texted Kate on the way over to double his tip and thank him for me. You're not moving fast enough."

"I'm in heels," she pointed out. "And you'd rather text someone else to thank him than take the time to do it yourself?"

He scooped her off her feet. "If it means I shaved a few seconds off of getting you out of this wedding dress, then yes, I'd much rather do that."

He didn't put her down again until they reached the room where he deposited her on the bed with a playful toss.

"What is with you and throwing me into beds, Mr. Sinclair."

He flipped her over and unzipped her dress. "Well, Mrs. Sinclair, I love you in this wedding dress, but I love you even more naked."

He had the dress off of her in seconds. And the time for joking soon came to end when he thrust into her from behind, his hips pumping into her in a blur of need. "You shouldn't have told me you weren't wearing any panties. You're lucky I didn't take you at the reception in front of all our guests."

Layla moaned, thrusting her butt backwards,

trying to take as much of him as she could, her own need wild and unhinged, as the sweetest sensation built inside of her womb, clenching her sex around his cock.

"So tight," Nathan said, pounding into her. "It's like you were designed for me, sweetheart." The orgasm hit them both on a crashing wave, washing over them, as Nathan's seed spilled into her.

"We made it," he said against the nape of her neck, his voice filled with awe. "You're finally mine."

"Now and forever," she said with a breathless laugh. "I love you."

"I love you." He pulled out and turned her over so she could see the sincerity in his eyes. "I love you now and forever. And I'm never going to let another day go by without telling you how much I love you. I promise you that."

Layla's answering smile lit up her entire face.

She believed he would keep that promise. She really did.

If you liked this story, check out the second book in the 50 Loving State Series:

<u>HER RUSSIAN BILLIONAIRE</u>

Theodora Taylor reads, writes, and reviews in Pittsburgh, Pennsylvania. When not reading, writing, or reviewing, she enjoys going to the movies, daydreaming, and attending dinner parties thrown by others with her wonderful husband. Feel free to contact her at <u>theodorawrites@gmail.com</u>, and if you love IR romance as much as she does, check out her review blog at <u>irbookreviews.com</u>